Stripped

STRIPPED: A FUN STRIPPER ROMANCE, REVERSE AGE GAP, SINGLE MUM NOVELLA.

C.SMITH

Copyright © [2024] by [C.Smith]

All rights reserved.

No part of this publication may be reproduced, distributed, or transmitted in any form or by any means, including photocopying, recording, or other electronic or mechanical methods, without the prior written permission of the author. For permission requests, contact [c.smith_books@outlook.com].

The story, all names, characters, and incidents portrayed in this production are fictitious. No identification with actual persons (living or deceased), places, buildings, and products is intended or should be inferred.

Book Cover by [C.Smith]

[First] edition [2024]

Contents

Trigger Warnings	V
Dedication	VII
1. Chapter One	2
2. Chapter Two	7
3. Chapter Three	11
4. Chapter Four	19
5. Chapter Five	25
6. Chapter Six	31
7. Chapter Seven	41
8. Chapter Eight	47
9. Chapter Nine	53
10. Chapter Ten	59
11. Chapter Eleven	67

12.	Chapter Twelve	75
13.	Chapter Thirteen	81
14.	Chapter Fourteen	89
15.	Chapter Fifteen	99
16.	Chapter Sixteen	107
17.	Epilogue	113
18.	What's Next...	117
19.	Finding Forever Series	118
20.	Acknowledgements	119
	About The Author	120

Trigger Warnings

Please be aware that Chapter Eleven contains content detailing experiences of sexual abuse, sexual assault, child neglect, violence, discussions of drug and alcohol abuse.

Note: The sexual abuse/assault detailed is NOT that of a child.

Please do skip this chapter if you feel it may be a trigger for you.

Foreword:

Due to the sexual nature and explicit content of this story, it is not recommended for readers under the age of 18.

Preface:

Stripped is set in 2019, five years before 'Lost And Found'.

Dedication

Sometimes a broken person just needs to be heard, be the person that listens.

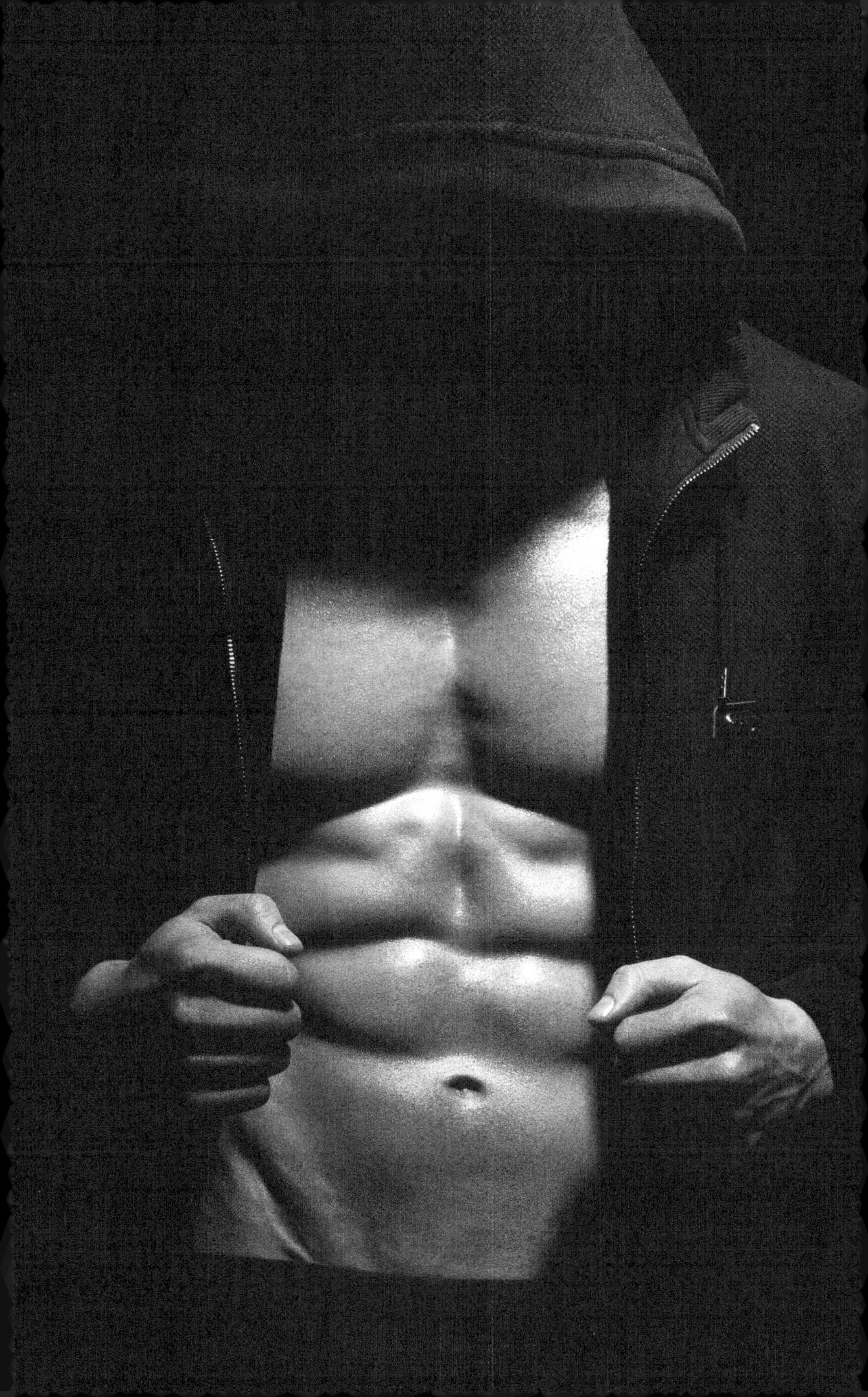

Chapter One

Jax

The music is pumping, the walls thumping with the pressure of the bass as I lather myself in oil. I'm wearing the tiniest pair of black boxer briefs known to man. My cock is hard as always and is trying to escape out of the top of my waistband. I totally get off on this shit. My heart is thumping a rhythm inside my chest as adrenaline courses through my body.

I'm currently twenty four years old and have been a stripper for the past two years. Now, I know it's not the most … wholesome way of making money but I love my job.

I'm not a bad looking dude and getting to spend every night with people wanting a piece of me isn't the worst way to spend my time. The money is bloody good too. Of course I don't want to be doing it forever but for now it keeps things ticking over.

See, I have this dream to own my own pub one day in Meadowside. I know right, how does a big town stripper become a small town pub landlord? Who knows. All I know is that's my goal and I'm going to get there one way or another.

Tonight's job though is to rub myself in oil, tease everybody with my hard cock while having cash thrown at me. Not a bad way to spend a few hours hey?

A knock sounds at the door just as I'm fixing my hair and checking there's nothing in my teeth,

"Two minutes Jax!" Mike the security guard shouts through the door.

"Coming!" I shout back. One quick spritz of aftershave. I quickly throw on my tight jeans and open white shirt, rolling my sleeves up to my elbows and head towards the stage.

Adrenaline is coursing through my body, I never feel nervous before a show, just excited. I love that moment when I walk out onto that stage and everybody starts screaming my name. It's addictive. It's confidence boosting and did I mention that it makes my cock hard?

I'm not entirely sure why it has such a strong effect on me. I've never been one to struggle to get the ladies attention. I'm tall, with dark brown hair which is longer on the top. Perfect for the ladies to grab a hold of and push me to my knees. I have pretty green eyes, so I've been told and I work out a lot. I'm well built, covered in tattoos and take a lot of pride in my appearance.

But for some reason, being lathered up in oil and taking my clothes off turns me on like mad.

The opening bars to Ginuwine - Pony starts playing, the strippers anthem. The screaming and chanting starts,

"Jax Jax Jax,"

I can't stop the smile that spreads across my face, feeling wanted feels pretty damn good. I can't say it was a feeling I was used to growing up. Having one ghost of a parent and the other an abusive arsehole, hadn't done my self esteem much good. Stripping had massively helped with that aspect of my life though.

I took a huge gulp of water and passed my bottle off to Mike before making my way to stand behind the curtain on stage. Three, two, one ... the curtain pulled back and everybody went wild. I couldn't hear myself think past the screaming.

My eyes flitted across the customers, checking out tonight's audience as I swaggered onto the stage and began to move. Bumping and grinding, the sweat began to trickle down my back as I slowly and teasingly pulled my shirt open and off my shoulders. I rubbed it down my sweaty chest and thrust my groin into it before throwing it blindly into the crowd.

Women fought each other for it, rubbing it all over themselves. Horny, drunk women were shameless and bloody hilarious. I was as sober as a judge, I never drank and I'd never done drugs. Having two addict parents had put me off for life. Funny that I wanted to own a pub though right. I'm not entirely sure why really, apart from maybe it would help me to hold a little bit of control and try to help people if I saw them struggling.

As much as I loved stripping and probably came across as an arrogant and cocky dude, I have a big heart to share with someone special one day. I care about people and would do anything to help someone in need.

Anyway, enough of the heavy thoughts. My mind moved back to the moment as I made my way to the floor and began grinding my hips into the stage, which was littered with cash already. My heart was thumping in my chest, sweat trickled down my body mixing with the oil.

I turned onto my back and began unbuttoning my jeans, my hard shaft pressing painfully against the zipper. I'd have to take care of that when I got off stage, or find someone pretty to take care of it for me.

I wouldn't say I was a playboy but if someone was offering, it'd be rude of me to turn them down right? Better than my right hand.

"Take it off, Take it off," the chanting continued as I slid the jeans over my arse and thrust slowly into the air.

I was hot, sweat pouring down my temples. Never mind, the next scene would cool me right off. I stood and made my way to the pole in the middle of the stage, grabbing a hold of it and moving my slick body against it. A couple of the workers quickly gathered my cash from the floor. A quick nod at Mike to the side and the water began trickling from the ceiling.

I stood underneath the warm shower of water as it trickled down my body and soaked straight through my jeans as I continued to work them down my thighs and kick them off into the crowd.

My boxers were soaked, the thick outline of my hard dick obviously visible as the audience went feral. I stroked my own hands down my wet body while dancing a slow rhythm under the waterfall, tipping my head back and letting the water soak my hair.

My hips ground into the air as I teasingly pulled at my waistband, opening my eyes to survey the audience once more. My eyes flitted across the crowd as I continued to move, before they stopped on the most beautiful woman I'd ever seen in my life.

Icy blonde hair pulled to one side over her shoulder, piercing blue eyes locked on mine. She was dressed in a gorgeous red skin tight dress showing off her ample cleavage. She sparkled with diamonds. Her pink pouty lips open with lust as she caressed my body with her eyes. My heart pounded in my chest and my cock grew even harder in my boxers, my tip poking out of the waistband as I continued to move my body under the spray of water.

The beauty's eyes lowered to my dick before finding my eyes again and licking her lips. I almost came in my pants right that second. Fuck!

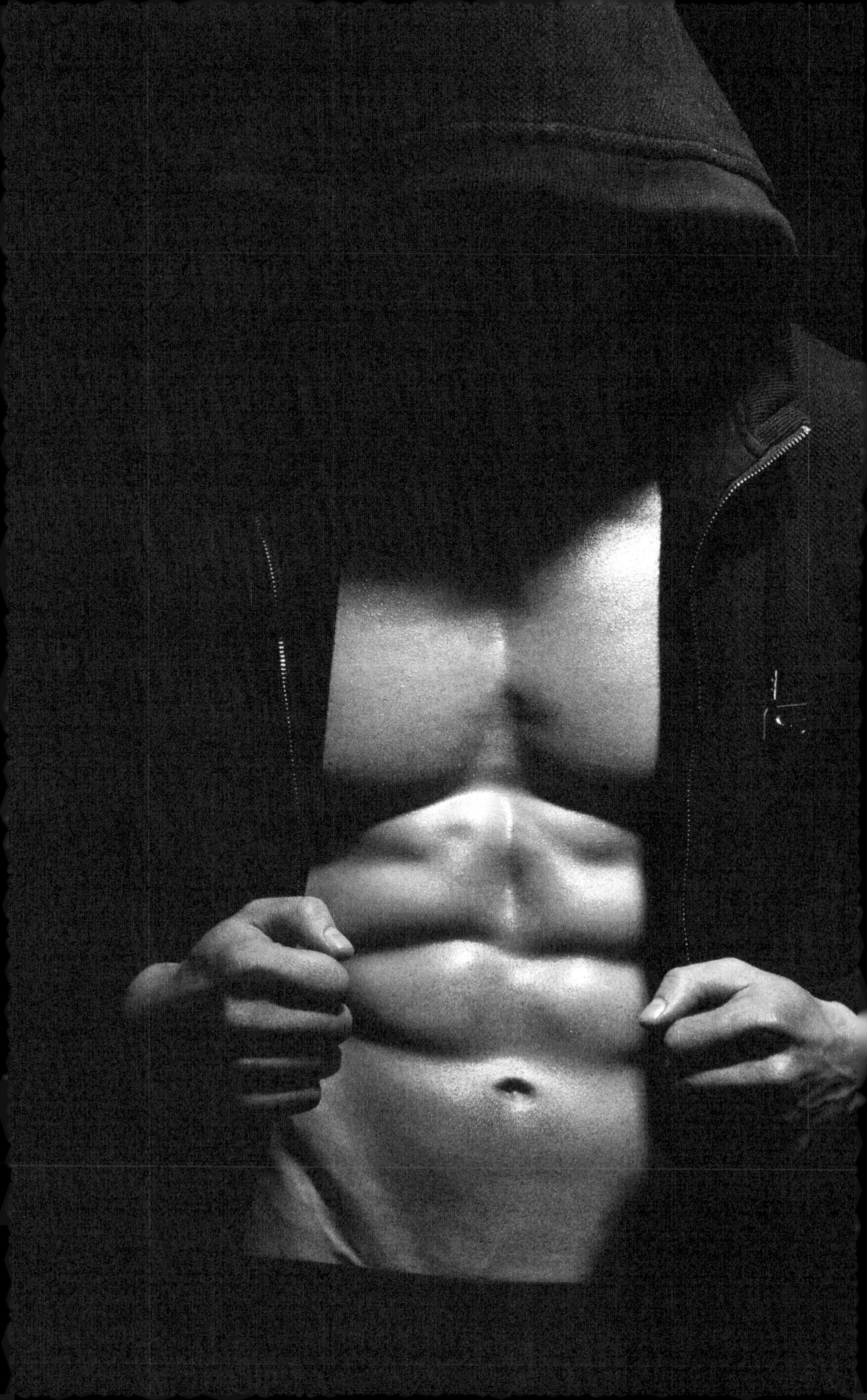

Chapter Two

Piper

Holy mother of hotness, this man was fine!

I'd never been to a strip club before but it was fair to say that I was hot, my body was buzzing and my panties were soaked. I'm sat at a table with my friends Paige and Hallie who are both drunk off their arses and heckling the poor man on stage. Not that he seems too bothered by it, he looks like he's having the time of his life.

From the moment he swaggered out onto that stage I haven't been able to take my eyes off of him. He's tall, maybe 6'2 at a guess. He has short brown hair, longer on the top which is flopping down across his forehead. He keeps pushing it back up and the way his arm muscles strain with the action is making my ovaries pulse.

He is gorgeous, a thick muscled chest leading down to an eight pack of abs and the most defined Adonis belt I've ever seen. He's covered in dark tattoos. I want to run my tongue across him.

I cannot seem to remove my eyes from this fine specimen of a man when his eyes lock on mine and I sit frozen, caught in his stare. His eyes caress my body, I can actually feel the tingles on my skin as he eats me up with his eyes. I shamelessly do the same to him, my eyes landing on … holy shit! That can't be real right? That is by far the biggest, thickest cock I've ever seen in my life and it's currently contained in the tiniest pair of boxer briefs. I can see the tip poking out of the top which causes me to lick my lips involuntarily. My eyes flit back to his quickly, shit! He caught me. He sends me a sexy wink before he gets back to his grinding.

Now stood in just his tiny boxers, he runs his big sexy hands up and down his body, teasing me, calling to me. The song is starting to come to an end and I absolutely do not want this moment to end. This sexy man standing under a waterfall of water, glistening, muscled, tattooed. He's like my very own wet dream come to life!

The crowd collectively holds it's breath as he reaching for the waistband of his boxers, leading quickly towards the end of his performance.

My heart is pounding in my chest, I can feel my heartbeat pounding in my panties as he looks me dead in the eyes with his pretty green ones. A grin spreads across his gorgeous face before he whips his boxers down and my jaw hits the floor. There's a moment of collective silence before the entire room erupts in excitement. Women are screaming, hooting, hollering. There are even a few guys celebrating this fine mans massive achievement! Paige and Hallie are screaming obscenities at him.

Meanwhile, I'm stunned silent, my eyes locked below the waist in a moment that seems to go on forever. In reality it only lasts a few seconds but I just cannot seem to take my eyes off of him. His beautiful hard cock, pointing up towards the skies. I wish I was close enough for a taste.

Time stays suspended until I finally move my gaze to his

eyes, a look of expectation passes in his expression. He tilts his head to the side, raising his eyebrows in a silent question. An invitation maybe and that scares the shit out of me and my hormones quickly plummet to the ground.

There's no way a God like that man would ever be interested in me, a thirty five year old divorcee with a ten year old daughter. I have stretch marks and cellulite, my boobs may look great in this dress but in reality breastfeeding my daughter all those years ago has destroyed them. I look tired, overworked and I couldn't tell you the last time I had a bikini wax.

It's those wayward thoughts that set my next actions in motion. The gorgeous man is still looking at me expectantly, hands now attempting to cover his crotch. As I get up from my seat, utter a quick goodbye to the girls and run towards the exit and out into the chilly night.

Jax

By the time I'd hurried off the stage and threw my wet boxers back on and followed her out into the night, she was gone.

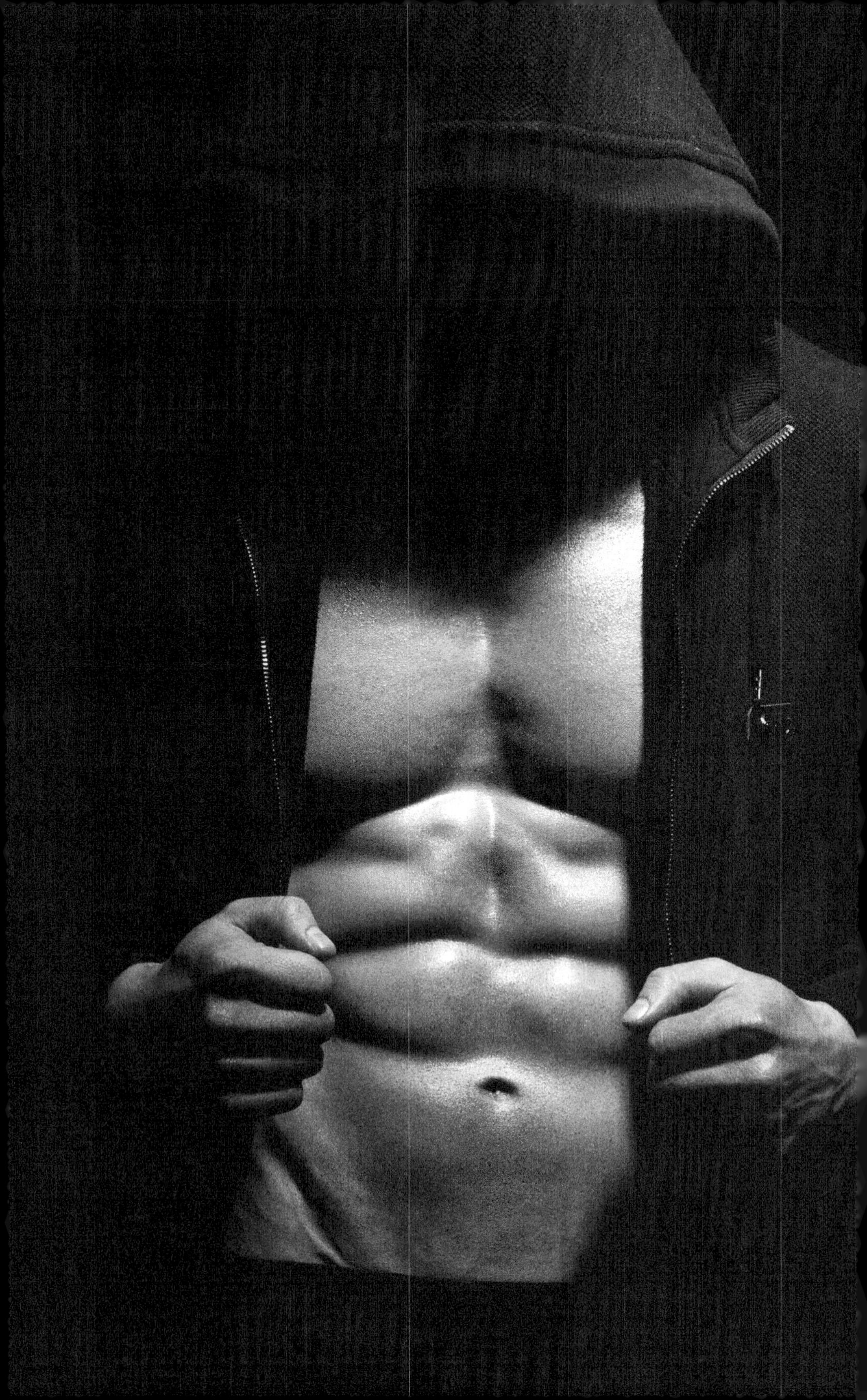

Chapter Three

Jax

It had been a week since I'd seen Blondie at my show and I hadn't seen her since. I'd hoped she would show up again but after the way she left, I hadn't been holding out much hope.

I hadn't meant to scare her away with my blatant invitation, she seemed as though she was as interested in me as I had been her. Maybe I'd been wrong, I wasn't known for toning down my behaviour but maybe I should have.

There was something about her that called to me, I hadn't been able to get her out of my mind since that night. That sinful red dress which was unveiled even more when she had stood up. She had a gorgeous hourglass figure, curves in all the right places and when she'd turned around and given me a view of that delectable arse. Holy hell, I had wanted to take a bite out of it and run my hands all over her.

I hadn't even managed to get her name. When I'd gone back inside to ask her friends about her, they were otherwise occupied with a group of young guys at the next table over.

I'd just have to try and forget about her.

    I was in Meadowside today helping my brother Ace move into his new place. Since we were kids we had always wanted to live in Meadowside. It was a quiet and peaceful little village on the English coast. It was perfect here. Rows of tiny cottages lined the streets and the Main Street was perfect. It only had the shops you'd need, not much choice if you fancied a shopping spree but to me it was perfect.

    Ace and I were from Bedgebury Place, the rough side of town. We'd grown up with two parents who were addicts, drugs and alcohol. My mother was a ghost and the only attention my father ever showed us was when he was beating the crap out of us. Most of the time we had to fend for ourselves, it was a miracle really that we were even alive.

    Ace was three years older than me and had always been a great big brother. He had protected me from more bullshit over the years than any kid ever should have had to. There were countless times when drug dealers were around our house, pounding on our Dad for owing them money.

    Or pimps around taking advantage of our Mother when Dad needed to earn some more money for their next fix. It was beyond fucked up and it was a miracle that Ace and I had turned out to be the decent human beings we were.

    I mean ... I know I stripped for money but that was only temporary. I had big dreams that I'd fulfil one day.

    So here we were, unloading the moving van and getting Ace's new home all set up. It was a tiny two bedroom cottage not far from the High Street. Ace had offered me his spare room but when I moved to Meadowside I wanted it to be because I'd worked hard to get here. And I would. One day.

I say 'we' were unloading the van, but it was me putting in most of the effort. Ace's phone was going off relentlessly, ding ding ding. It was doing my head in. The dinging would sound and then Ace would double over cackling like an old witch.

"Dude, are you going to help or what? I'm not carrying all your shit in here if you're not going to help!" I told him with a frown.

"Oh shut it you miserable sod, I'm helping. I can't help it that my friends are funnier than yours".

The truth was I didn't really have many friends, only the other guys and girls at the club. Despite being a hit with the ladies, I'd otherwise always been a bit of a loner and I was fine with that. One day I'd find my people.

We spent hours moving all of Ace's shit into his new house, before we knew it the sun was going down and my stomach was growling.

"Mate I'm starving, let's get something to eat".

"Sure thing," Ace replied. "Hugh is on his way round with the boys, he's bringing chinese food".

I gave him a nod, I liked Ace's friends. They had always made me feel like part of the group.

Hugh, Mack, and Ryan arrived a little while later and the food was inhaled in a matter of mere minutes. That's when the invasive questioning started, like it always did.

"So, how's the job going?" Hugh asked. He had always been supportive of what I'd done, we all had to make ends meet after all. He had a gorgeous pregnant wife at home called Grace and he was generally a pretty serious dude.

"Yeah, it's going," I replied. "I've managed to save up quite a bit now, I reckon maybe a few more months and I may have enough to get out of there".

"That's great news mate, I'm pleased for you. Did you hear that Louie is selling the pub in the village? He's decided to retire soon". Hugh told me.

"Oh really? That would be the perfect place. Maybe I'll pop by on my way home tomorrow," I replied. I was staying over at Ace's tonight as it had been a long day.

"Jax?" Mack asked, he was like a little puppy dog. Sweet, shy and one hundred percent devoted to his new wife Maisie.

"Yeah?" here we go.

"I totally support your job choice and everything, but, is it not weird getting your cock out every night?" he said it so straight faced and serious that the rest of us couldn't hold back the laughter that burst out of us. Ace was bent over, pounding his hand on his knee dramatically. He was such an attention seeker.

After I managed to catch my breath, I told him,

"At first it was super weird. Standing in front of a room full of horny chicks and dudes staring at my junk. Pretty quickly though I realised that they loved me and that shit is pretty good as a confidence boost!" I laughed.

"I just don't think I could do it. Plus Maisie would chop my balls off with a rusty bread knife that's for sure," Mack said with a wince.

"That's understandable. If I was ever to be lucky enough to fall in love then I'd stop the stripping instantly. I wouldn't like other men leering at my woman so I wouldn't expect her to be ok with me doing it".

"How very noble" Ryan piped up. He was younger than the rest of us, he had just turned twenty two. He was a fire-fighter alongside the other guys. Now that's a job I don't think I'd be able to do, putting myself in danger everyday? Nope, I'll stick to getting my cock out thanks.

"Speaking of ladies," Hugh started. "You met anyone special recently Jax?".

"Me?" I pointed to my chest. "Women only want me for a good time, not much else. Although, I did …" I trailed off.

Nope, that would be a bad idea to tell them about Blondie.

Ace was like a dog with a bone and I'd never hear the end of it.

"What did you do?" My brother piped up. I heaved a breath, did I really want to tell them? I could probably do with some manly advice. Ah screw it, what's the worst that could happen.

"Well, last week while I was working there was this woman in the crowd. She was … God she was beautiful. She couldn't take her eyes off me and I was drawn to her like a magnet. Once I'd finished my set, I was going to go over and talk to her but she literally ran out of the club. By the time I'd put my cock away she was gone. I've not seen her since. I don't even know her name". I told them.

The boys were so laser focussed on my face I felt like I was under a microscope being observed.

"You've never been hung up on a woman before," Ace stated the obvious. He was right, I was a one and done kind of dude. I didn't want to be but I'd never met anybody who had been able to hold my attention and see more than just 'Jax The Stripper'.

"I know," I said quietly, taking a sip of my beer.

"What does she look like?" Ryan asked.

"Well, it was pretty hard to see in the dark club but she had long icy blonde hair. Piercing blue eyes, a body made to do very dirty things. Curvy, petite, gorgeous. She was with two other women. I'd say she was probably older than me but not by much. She was … perfect".

I was pretty hung up on her and it was so damn stupid, I hadn't even gotten the chance to talk to her.

"She sounds nice mate," Mack spoke up. "You never know, she may show up again".

"I hope so mate, I hope so".

We finished our beers, said goodbye to the guys before heading up to bed. I then spent the next ten minutes with my hand wrapped around my hard dick as I imagined piercing blue eyes, icy blonde hair and rosy pink lips.

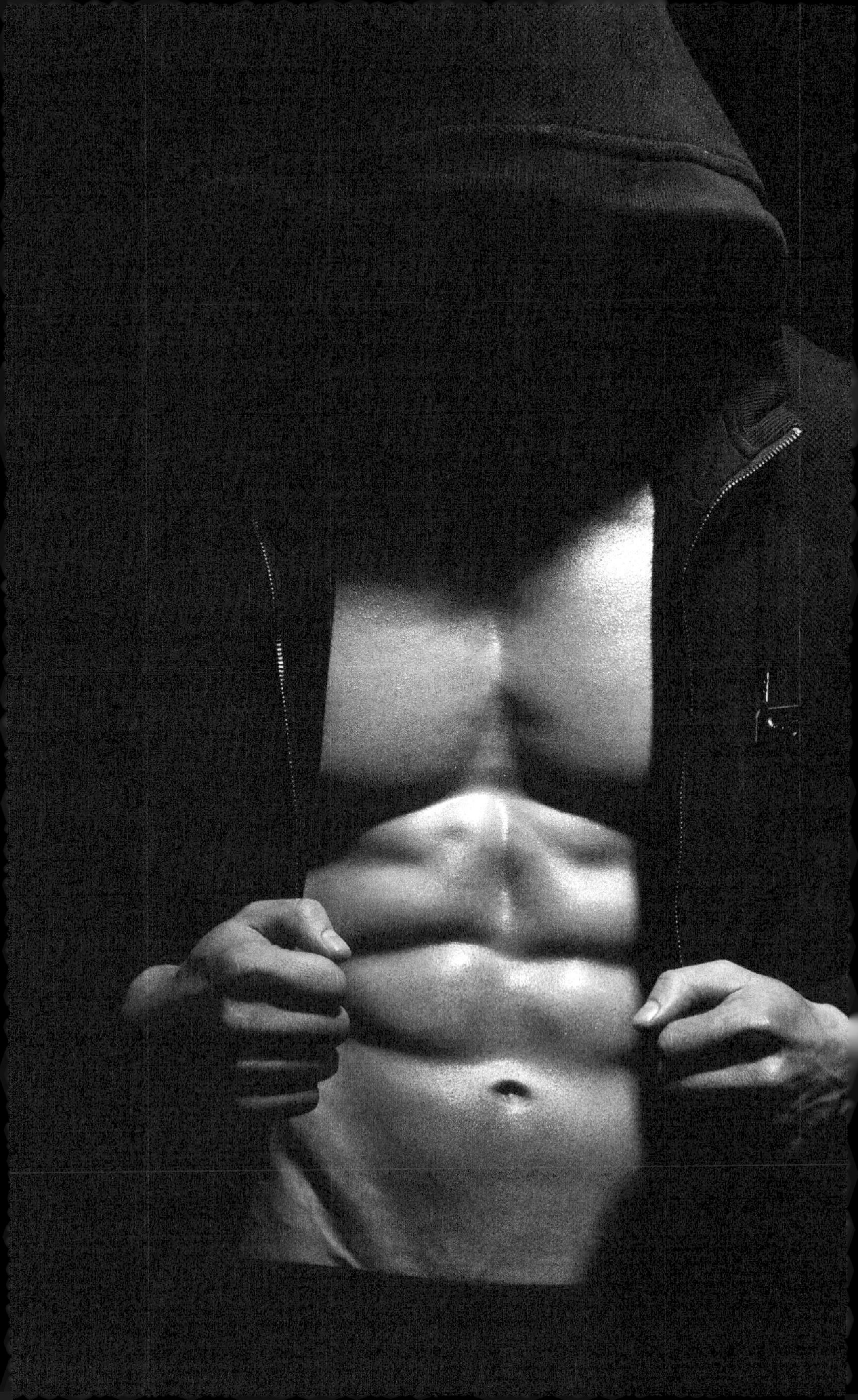

Chapter Four

Piper

I had just settled behind my desk at work when our new vet Maisie came bounding through the door. She was a fiery redhead and I had taken to her instantly. She was twenty seven years old, had a lovely husband called Mack and she was mental. In the best way possible. She was feisty and loyal and made me belly laugh like nobody else.

She was unapologetically herself and if you didn't like it then quite frankly you could fuck off. I was eight years older than her but I wanted to be Maisie when I grew up. I'd do anything to be a bit more like her, not caring about what anybody else thought. Maybe then I wouldn't be currently regretting my recent decisions and I would have taken that gorgeous man to bed!

He was still on my mind, Jax. I only knew his first name but I couldn't get that sweaty body out of my mind. That wet, muscled, tattooed body and that giant cock. God I missed getting laid. I hadn't been with anybody since Robbie, we divorced last year. But my God did I wish I'd bedded Jax.

He was right there, all naked, hard and inviting. But I chickened out like a total coward because of my own insecurities. If only I didn't have the body of a thirty five year old mother, then I would have jumped his bones without a second thought.

"Piper?"

"Piper?"

"Earth to Piper …" Maisie was talking and I had completely switched off whilst imagining what those muscles would look like from below, watching him as he thrust into me. Holy shit, I needed to calm the fuck down. Jeez.

"Sorry … what?" I asked breathlessly.

"I said … are you ok? You look like you're having some kind of medical emergency?" Maisie smirked.

"I'm fine," I said with a laugh. "Just got some things on my mind".

"They looked like some pretty good things, care to share?" Maisie asked with a wicked smile on her face, whilst rubbing her hands together. I contemplated telling her, she was younger than me and much closer to Jax's age I would assume. Although, this felt like such a stupid situation. I am a thirty five year old mother. What right did I have to be lusting over a twenty something. My insecurities were grating on me, it was time to be a bit more like Maisie.

"Well … oh God you're going to laugh your arse off at me," My face hit my palm as I tried to hide behind my hands.

"Nope, come on. Time to share," Maisie took a seat on the other side of my desk, resting her feet up on the table. If it had been anyone else it would have annoyed the hell out of me. But something tells me that Maisie knew how to get her own way, she's so …. lovable. Not entirely sure if that's the right word but that's what I'm going with. I took a deep breath and word vomit spewed from my mouth like a geyser.

"Last week I went to a strip club with Paige and Hallie.

There was an insanely gorgeous guy there, all sexy and sweaty. He was one of the dancers obviously. I cannot get this man out of my mind! He's younger than me, by a lot I think. At the end of his dance he looked at me, it felt like an invitation".

Maisie was sat forward, hands steepled under her chin completely enraptured with my sad story.

"And then what happened? You did didn't you? Please tell me you took that man up on his offer?".

"No," I told her with a sigh and laid my head down on the table, "I completely chickened out and ran out of the club, as I drove away in my car I saw him standing outside in his boxers looking for me. He followed me out and I just drove away like a total coward".

"Why did you run though Pipes?" Maisie asked, sympathy in her tone.

"Well look at me," I sat up and gestured down my body "Why the hell would a twenty something year old man that looked like that, want anything to do with me? I'm thirty five years old with saggy boobs and cellulite, I have stretch marks and a podgy belly. I have a ten year old child. Even my own husband didn't want me. He could probably get any woman he wanted. Obviously the lighting wasn't very good in the club and he wasn't able to see me properly". I couldn't stop the tear that left my eye. I'd always had hang ups about my body which had only gotten worse once I'd had Posie.

Robbie had never been overly interested in me. I mean, I knew he loved me but that was about familiarity I think. He finally got bored of me and fucked his young, hot secretary. Total cliché I know.

"Now hold the fuck up," Maisie almost shouted at me as she stood and rounded the table, coming to stand right in front of me. She grabbed my face in both of her hands and turned me towards her. "You are the hottest thirty five year old MILF I've ever seen. If I was into women then I'd totally do you". She said with a smirk.

"You are gorgeous Piper, with that gorgeous blonde hair and blue eyes. You're every mans dream. Any man would be lucky to have you, regardless of their age. You have a rocking body baby and it's about time you flaunted it. It sounds like this dude was super interested? And Robbie can fuck right off and carry on fucking his way around town. It's his loss, you're the jackpot baby!". She pulled me into a hug and used her fingers to swipe away my tears.

"Anyway, do you know anything about this hottie from the club? A name or anything?" She asked.

"Well I only know his first name. If it's his real name of course, he might use a stage name," I paused, remembering those gorgeous eyes that pinned me to my seat. "His name was Jax".

Maisie looked at me with wide eyes, her jaw almost hitting the floor. She stood frozen for almost twenty whole seconds, I almost poked her before she burst out,

"Holy fucking shit!".

Twenty minutes later she came bounding back into the room like an overly excited puppy, luckily I was between patients.

"Right, you have a blind date tonight my lovely. Seven o'clock you are to be in Louie's pub, wearing a blue dress. Mack and I are coming to sit with Posie. No more of this sulking. You are going to go out there and show the god damn world what a total knockout you are. Thank you … and goodbye!". She turned and stalked out of the room before I'd even gotten the chance to reply.

It took a few seconds to pick my jaw up off the floor as I stared after her, before I decided what the hell. Might as well make use of a mid week babysitter. Even if I end up sitting in Louie's all by myself.

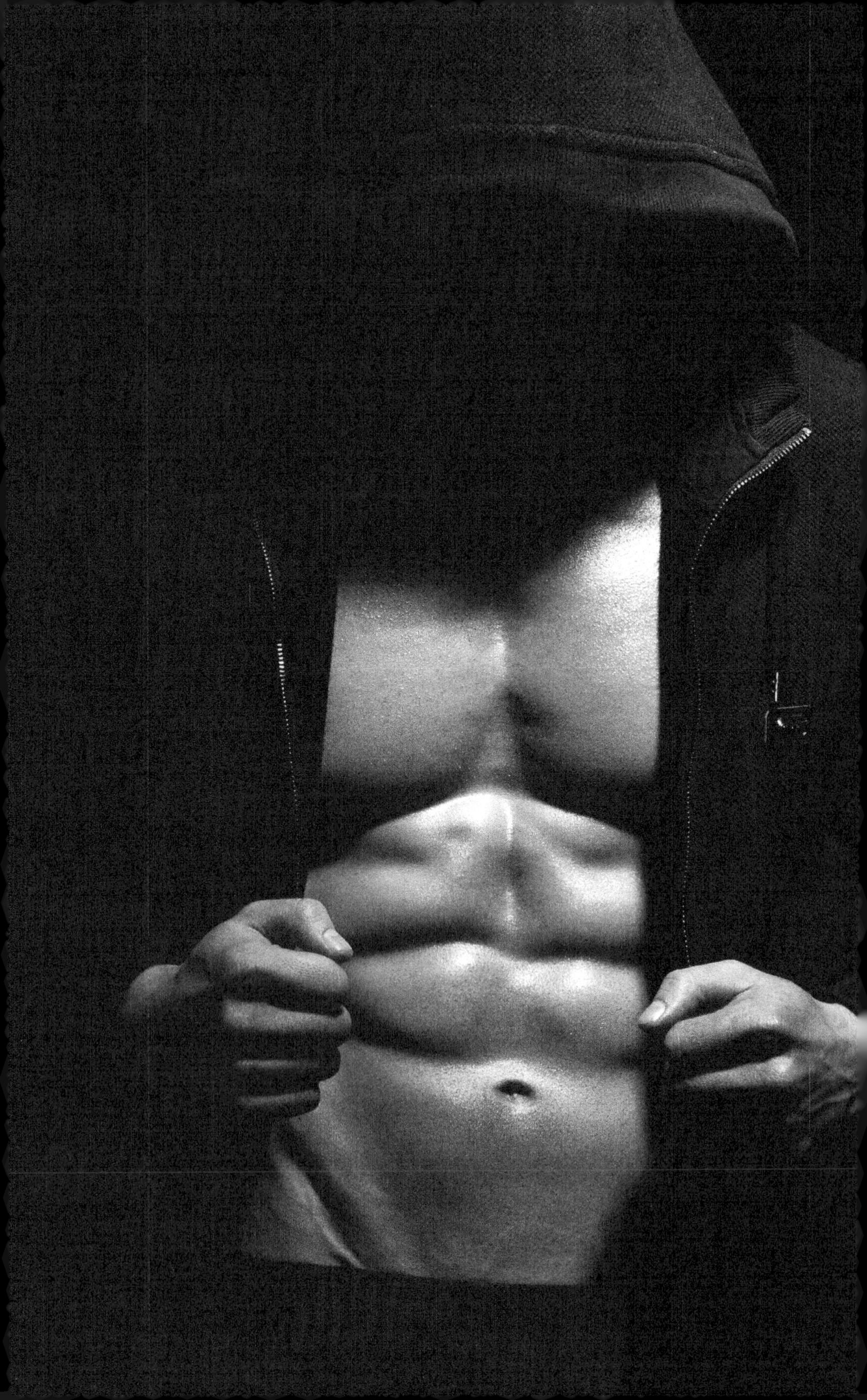

Chapter Five

Jax

I'd just had the most random text message from Mack. He had never even messaged me before so I wasn't entirely sure how he'd gotten my number but that's neither here nor there.

It was all very random, I was to go to Louie's in Meadowside tonight at seven o'clock for a blind date. This had Ace's name written all over it, that dick never knew when to leave well enough alone. I didn't need to be set up, I didn't need help to find a woman.

I wasn't working tonight though so figured what the hell, might as well go along. Even if it's just for the company, it would be pretty nice not to have to eat dinner by myself for once.

With that thought in my mind, I jumped into the shower and got myself ready to go, it was a damn shame I still couldn't get those gorgeous blue eyes out of my mind.

I walked into Louie's at exactly seven o'clock. It was a major pet peeve of mine when someone was late. As if I had nothing better to do than sit around waiting for someone else. Luckily my date in question obviously had the same thoughts on tardiness as I could see her waiting for me at the bar.

Mack had said that I was to look out for a woman wearing a blue dress, she would be waiting for me at the bar. He hadn't even told me her name and I hadn't thought to ask, I wasn't particularly interested if I'm being honest. Never mind, I was here now and couldn't stop myself from checking this woman out.

She had long blonde hair, pulled over her shoulder in some sort of twist thing. She was wearing a tight blue dress that hugged her curves and stopped at her knees and she had on a pair of fuck me heels that were so high. She was still tiny though, she'd probably only reach my shoulder. My eyes raked up and down her body from behind, her gorgeous heart shaped arse looked good enough to eat.

I had just started walking towards her thinking that maybe this wasn't the worst idea in the world when she must have sensed me coming, she turned to face me. Her eyes starting at my feet and raking up my body, blatantly checking me out. I was doing the same to her. That was until our eyes clashed and a flash of recognition passed between us.

I knew her immediately, I'd dreamed of that sinful body, those piercing eyes and having that blonde hair wrapped around my wrist as I took her from behind. It was Blondie, she was here. How the hell was that possible? We literally stood staring at each other for long seconds before I finally managed to get my brain to work and my mouth to move.

"Blondie? Is that you?" I asked.

"Blondie?" She quirked an eyebrow and gave me a smirk.

I huffed out a small laugh, "I never got the chance to learn your name before you left".

"Piper ... my name is Piper".

"It's great to meet you Piper", I leaned forward to press my lips to her cheek in greeting, resting a hand on her arm. She was warm and smelled like coconut. The scent hit me instantly and went right to my dick, making me harder than concrete in my jeans.

"It's nice to meet you too, Jax? You're real name is Jax?" she questioned breathlessly.

"Yeah, I'm Jax ... How are you here right now? How did Mack do this?". I asked Piper, her name was beautiful.

"Mack?" Piper paused before giggling out loud, it was a beautiful sound. "Mack, as in Maisie's Mack?".

I nodded before she continued, "That conniving little ... I work with Maisie, I had told her about you. I can't believe she managed to find you. How did she find you?".

"Mack is friends with my brother Ace, funnily enough I was telling them about you too, how I wished you hadn't run off that night". Sadness and a dash of guilt flashed across her face.

"Come on, let's go and eat. We can chat". She reached out her hand which I took eagerly in mine, before leading me to the table that was waiting for us.

We enjoyed the next hour or so, making small talk, getting to know each other whilst eating a delicious meal. Something was bugging me though and I just knew it wouldn't stop until I asked her. I had nothing to lose so I just blurted it out.

"Why did you run away that night? I thought we shared a ... moment".

Piper took a deep breath, scrubbed her tiny hands down her face before looking me in the eye and telling me with complete honesty ...

"I chickened out. I'm sorry. We did share a moment and believe me when I tell you that I have wished every day since that I had taken you up on your offer. It's just that, well ...".

She looked so uncertain, nerves flashing across her face. She was fidgeting in her seat as a blush crept up her neck to her cheeks. I didn't like the thought of making her nervous, which led me to reach across the table and take her hands in mine.

"You can tell me anything", I murmured. She gave me a small nod in response.

"You are just so ... fucking gorgeous", I couldn't help but smirk, "And I'm ... me. I'm quite obviously a lot older than you. I have a child, I'm not a fit and firm twenty something Jax. You're way out of my league. How could someone like you possibly be interested in someone like me?".

I sat in shock, a frown marring my forehead, there was no way that this woman seriously thought I was out of her league.

"What? You're not serious?", I asked her in disbelief. Another small nod was all she gave me. I shook my head in shock.

"Piper, you are the most beautiful woman I've ever seen in my life. When I saw you sat in the audience at my show I was drawn to you like a moth to a flame. You are absolutely stunning, your body is to die for and quite frankly I'd take you right here and now if we weren't in this busy pub. I've never seen anyone quite like you before", I meant every single word. Proof of that was the fact that I hadn't been able to stop thinking about Piper since I met her, I told her the same.

"My mind has been stuck on you since I saw you that night. I can't get you out of my head. I thought I'd never see you again. And the age thing, who even cares about age? You can't be that much older than me, a couple years. How old are you?". I asked gently.

"I'm thirty five Jax, I have a ten year old daughter and I'm a divorcee".

"Eleven years ... we have eleven years between us?", I almost whispered, not because I was put off or embarrassed. But because there was something about it that turned me the fuck on.

"Yeah," Piper said with a sigh. "It's alright, I understand". She looked so sad, like she truly believed she was anything other than a total smoke show.

"No," I told her firmly. "You don't understand, let me ask you one question and depending on your answer then there's something I want to show you, ok?.

"Yeah ... yeah ok", she replied.

"That night, in the club. If it wasn't for your insecurities and the things you've just told me about, would you? Would you have come home with me?".

She didn't even have to think about it, the answer was out of her mouth and flung into the atmosphere around us.

"Yes, no doubt about it".

I was up and out of my chair in a flash, grabbing her by the hand and hauling her out of the pub. Luckily I'd already settled the bill. I couldn't wait a second longer to show this stunning woman just how desirable she really was.

I hoped she was ready for me.

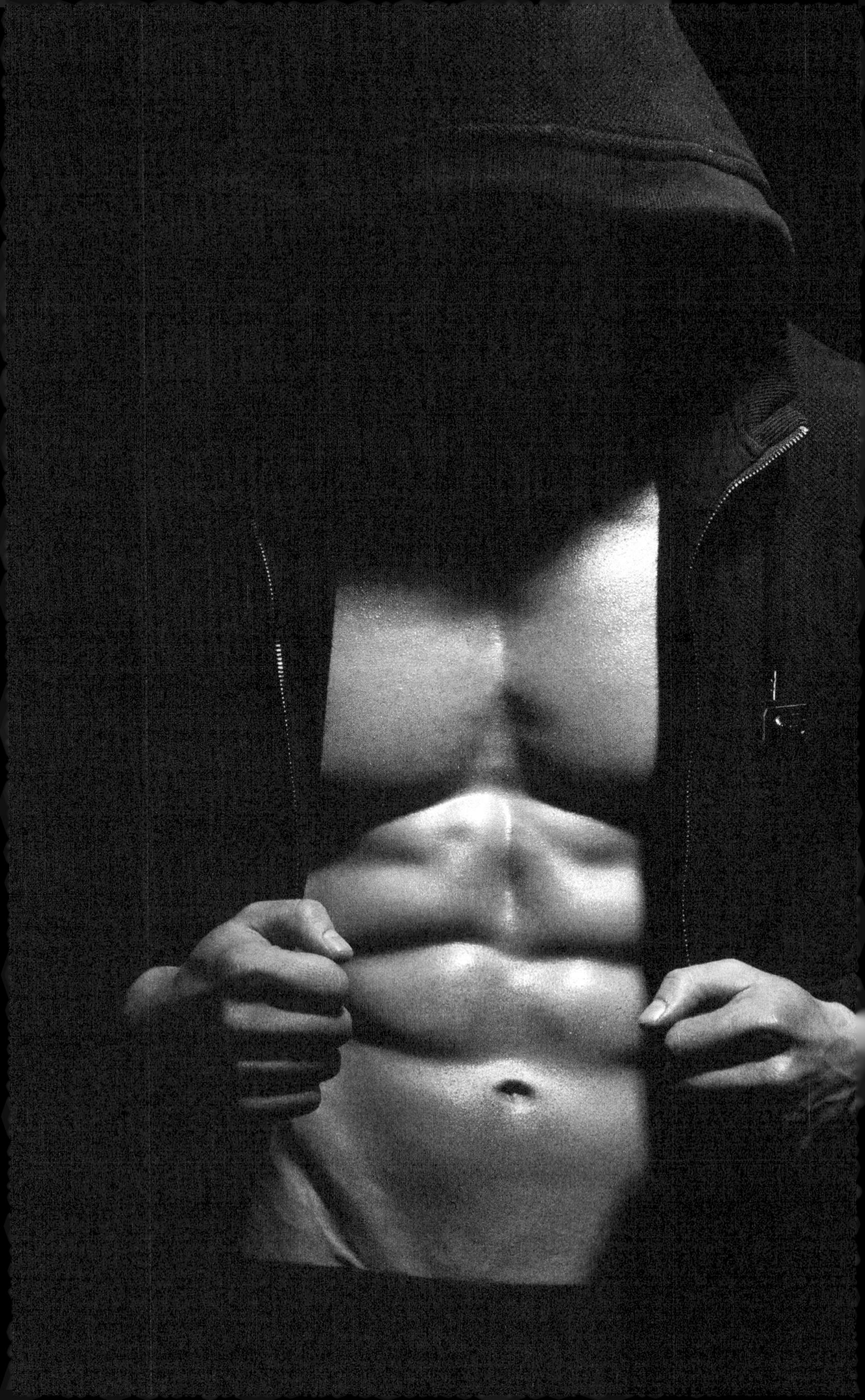

Chapter Six

Piper

    Jax grabbed me by the hand with a wicked grin plastered across his face, I had no idea what he was up to but here I was going along with it anyway. He pulled me along behind him as he weaved in and out of the tables before reaching the front door of the restaurant we had just eaten in.
    He stopped abruptly and turned to face me,
    "Last chance Blondie ... you sure?" I knew by the mischievous look on his face that we weren't talking about wholesome, PG fun here. That little voice in the back of my head continued to niggle at me but I was determined to ignore it. Jax had given me absolutely no indication that he didn't find me one hundred percent attractive. I didn't know how the hell that was possible but I was intent on channelling my inner Maisie and taking the bull by the horns so to speak.
    "Yes, I'm sure", I told him with a sharp nod.
    The smile that graced his face should be illegal, he looked so young and ... naughty. That was the only way to describe

that look, he looked like he was about to do very naughty things and I was here for it.

"You asked for it", he said before pulling me down the pavement. His huge warm hand was clasped in mine, electricity shot up my arm causing goose bumps to pebble across my skin. Butterflies were fluttering in my tummy, my breath was coming in quick bursts. I'd never felt so excited and free.

We were almost running, laughter pouring from us before we came to an abrupt stop. I nearly flew right into Jax's back, luckily he turned just in time to catch me in his arms. We froze, staring into each others eyes. My entire body was buzzing, Jax's lips were millimetres away, I could smell his rich aftershave. We were both heaving giant breaths while pressed together, chest to chest.

A low rumble sounded from his chest before he lowered me to the ground and ushered me inside the photobooth we'd stopped beside. What was he up to? I had to wonder. Jax sat down first on the tiny bench before gesturing me to take a seat on his lap. For a fraction of a second I hesitated, I was too heavy to sit on his lap. I didn't want him to feel my weight.

Jax picked up on my hesitation immediately as he patted his thigh and told me,

"Don't overthink it. Come and take a seat milady". With that charming smile across his face, how could I ever say no.

I entered the photobooth and gingerly lowered myself onto the end of his knees, but that wasn't good enough for my sexy friend here. Nope, he grabbed me by the waist and pulled me back against his body. He was firm, muscled and holy mother of orgasms, he was rock solid beneath me. Hard and huge. I'd seen that cock on stage, granted I hadn't been very close to the stage but it was damn near impossible to miss. It was currently nestled against my arse. Jax couldn't hold back the groan that left his throat before quickly busying himself with the photobooth screen.

He set it up ready to go before meeting my eyes in our reflection,

"Say cheese", he murmured. At the very last second, while the camera robot was counting down, Jax grabbed a hold of my chin, turned my head and slammed his lips to mine. Wow, his lips were soft and firm and he instantly demanded entry into my mouth. The kiss started off slow and exploratory but soon built into an inferno of passion.

He grabbed my rolling hips and pulled me flush against his hard length. Our lips never left each others as we continued to grind into each other. Jax pulled back, his chest heaving before he demanded,

"Turn around", I immediately obeyed. The chemistry in the air was electric, we could barely take a breath in this tiny photobooth. Luckily it was gone ten o'clock at night so hopefully nobody would be waiting to use it.

I stood and turned around to face Jax, looking into his lust filled eyes as my heart began to race faster in my chest. He brought his hands to the backs of my thighs and began to run his fingertips down to the hem of my dress and up again. I was soaking wet for him already, one small touch had me ready to jump this man.

He brought those lust filled green eyes back up to mine, a silent quest for permission in his eyes. I couldn't believe that this man wanted to touch me. I must be dreaming. I had to make sure I wrung out every inch of pleasure before I woke up.

"Yes", I whispered breathlessly.

Jax's eyes closed on an exhale before he rested his forehead against my stomach and immediately began pulling up the hem of my dress. His warm hands covered the backs of my thighs as his fingers pushed into my bare arse cheeks. He groaned against my body as he lowered his face to my sex and took a deep inhale.

"Fuck Blondie, you smell divine. I need a taste", meanwhile

I was preparing to spontaneously combust and turn into a puddle on the floor.

Jax didn't hold back a second longer as he sharply pulled my dress up high above my waist. Baring my black lace g-string to him. He stroked his fingers softly down the front of my sex before slipping a finger beneath the fabric and pulling it to the side. I was bared to him, soaked for him.

"Jesus Blondie, you're dripping for me". He swiped a thick finger through my wetness before bringing his glistening finger up to his mouth and sucking my juices with a hum.

Next thing I knew, my g-string was being lowered down my legs, I step out of them before bending to pick them up to put in my purse. Jax beat me to it, as soon as I had them in my hand he grabbed them with his and pushed them into the back pocket of his jeans.

"These are mine now". He muttered seconds before his mouth descended on me. He pressed soft kisses from my belly button all the way down to my bare slit. I always felt more comfortable completely bare down there and I was thankful for my last minute decision to go for a much needed and long awaited wax this afternoon before my date.

Jax seemed to approve as he grabbed one of my legs and raised it to rest on the bench beside him, before shifting forward and lowering himself to his knees in front of me. I couldn't help the moan that escaped, this man looked good on his knees. Without a second more to waste, he lowered his mouth and devoured me like a starving man.

He nipped and sucked at my clit as he pushed his thick fingers inside of me. I grabbed a hold of his hair with both hands, my hips were grinding relentlessly into his face. He had one big hand on my arse, two thick fingers deep inside me and his sinful tongue going to town on my pussy. Warmth began to flood my veins, tightening uncoiled in my stomach as my orgasm hit and I flooded this mans mouth.

"Fuck yeah", Jax muttered against my skin, "Drench me

Blondie". When I finally came back down to earth, my need for this man hadn't dissipated at all. I grabbed a hold of his shoulders and dragged him back up onto the bench before lowering to my knees in front of him. The cold metal floor dug into my knee caps but I didn't care. I just needed to bring him as much pleasure as he'd given me. I'd never been a huge fan of giving a blow job before but at this moment I just needed this man in my mouth.

"Take it out", I breathlessly moaned while clawing at Jax's belt. He didn't keep me waiting. He undid his belt, lowered his zipper and lifted just enough to lower his jeans and boxer briefs below his arse, freeing his ginormous ... holy fuck ... ginormous pierced cock. How the hell did I miss that the other night.

He was huge, at least ten inches. He was thick and hard and leaking at his tip. All of my confidence suddenly drained from my body. I wanted him more than anything but seriously, look at this guy.

"No more thinking baby, let loose. Do whatever you want to do to me. I want you, you're the most stunning woman I've ever met. Equally, if you've changed your mind then that's fine too". He grabbed the base of his cock, squeezing firmly to dissipate the ache. It looked painful.

I looked up into his eyes, sincerity shone back at me. He meant it, he meant every word he'd just said. He wants me, not some other woman. He wants me. My resolve snapped back into place, I could do this, I wanted this man.

Without a second more to hesitate, I took him in my hand. He was thick and warm. Rock solid and weeping. I lowered my head and swiped my tongue across his slit, licking up his salty come. Before opening wide and taking him all the way to the back of my throat.

He groaned loudly as he took my hair in his hands, creating a ponytail on the back of my head as he watched me intently. His eyes were hooded as he dropped his chin to his chest and began to move his hips, pushing himself further into my throat. I was intensely grateful for my lack of a gag reflex. Pleasuring this man made me feel a power I'd never felt before. Watching him begin to come in front of my eyes was like a drug.

It was bringing me to the precipice of another orgasm myself. I wanted Jax inside of me, I wondered if he wants to be there too? I hadn't realised I'd stopped moving until Jax placed his hand around the front of my throat and squeezed gently, making my eyes raise to him.

"You ok?", he barely choked out. The poor man was hanging on by a thread.

I nodded around his length before letting him fall from my mouth and standing abruptly in front of him.

"I want you", I was breathless. I barely recognised my own voice.

"I want you too Blondie, more than I've ever wanted anything in my life", he told me sweetly before standing and taking my lips with his. Kissing me for long seconds, not caring at all that I'd just had his cock in my mouth. He eventually pulled back a fraction, before asking,

"Here?".

"Yes, I can't wait any longer. I need you right now".

"I don't have a condom, I didn't think we would end up in this .... situation", a smirk pulled at his mouth.

"I don't care, I'm on birth control and I trust you. I want you".

"Then you can have me, I'm clean I promise".

"Me too", I muttered. In truth, I hadn't been with anybody since my divorce last year.

My words caused him to move into action, gone was nice, sweet Jax. In his place was dominating Jax. He grabbed my hips and turned me around so that I was facing the wall. We were still in this tiny photobooth, a thin curtain our only privacy from the world.

"Hands on the wall", Jax told me. I obeyed immediately.

He moved in closer, pressing his chest into my back before peppering soft kisses down my neck and across my naked shoulders.

And then I felt him, his hard length swiping back and forth across my wetness. The cold snap of his piercing knocking against my clit and stealing all the air from my lungs.

He notched himself at my entrance and pushed inside, slowly, inch by inch before his hips sat flush against my arse and I felt more full than I'd ever felt in my life.

"Holy shit, you're huge". I shuddered against him and involuntarily clenched, pulling him impossibly deeper into my body.

"Fuck, you're so tight. I need to move", his voice was gravelly, he was barely holding on.

I pushed my arse back into him as he began to move, sliding his thickness in and out of me. His piercing massaging my inner walls. My orgasm began to quickly build. Each thrust bringing me closer and closer to the most powerful climax I'd ever experienced.

He was relentless, his hard thrusts punishing. The sounds of our skin slapping against one another and our harsh breaths were the only sounds filling the small place.

Warmth began to spread across my body, white lights flashed behind my eyes as I exploded. My pussy clenched, pulling him deeper as I screamed into my own hand.

"Can I?", he could barely form a sentence, "Can I? Inside you?".

"Yes, yes, yes!", I met him thrust for thrust before he stilled and spilled his seed deep inside me. Pulse after pulse of hot come filling me and beginning to seep out and run down my inner thighs.

"Holy fuck Blondie, it's never felt like that before. I think I just died and came back to life again", he nuzzled his face into my neck whilst he tried to calm his breathing. I couldn't help the vulnerability that flooded me, the intense need to be held by him. He seemed to know what I needed before I could even tell him as he gathered me into his arms and pulled me back into his chest. Holding me tightly, filling me with feelings I'd never felt before.

"Me too", I whispered. I couldn't believe we had just done that. It was so unlike me. It had been the best night of my life.

Once we caught our breath and managed to get our clothes back on, all whilst crammed into the tiny photobooth. Jax pulled me into his arms and kissed me softly.

"I need to see you again beautiful. I don't know what the hell that was but I need more of it. Can I see you again? Please?". He was so vulnerable in that moment, there was absolutely no way I could refuse him and I wouldn't want to. Whatever happened between us in that photobooth had been explosive, our chemistry was off the charts. Our connection was undeniable, I felt like I'd known him for years. I needed to see him again too.

"I'd like that", I told him with a shy smile. We exchanged numbers with the promise to text tomorrow before leaving the photobooth hand in hand. Thankfully there was nobody about. Just as we started walking away, the photobooth let out a beep and the sound of photos printing filled the air around us.

Our eyes immediately met, the look of disbelief passed between us before we both burst into a fit of laughter in the middle of the street. Jax was laughing so hard, he had to put his hands on his knees for stability. Tears of laughter were streaming down both of our faces as the photobooth beeped twice and spat out five long strips of photos.

We almost pushed each other out of the way as we ran to retrieve them. Jax grabbed them quickly and held them up for us both to see, the breath left my lungs as I took in the sight before me.

Right there, in print, was our entire encounter. Jax on his knees, me on mine and finally Jax pressed up against my back as he watched his hard cock disappear inside of me.

Shit ... what a fucking night!

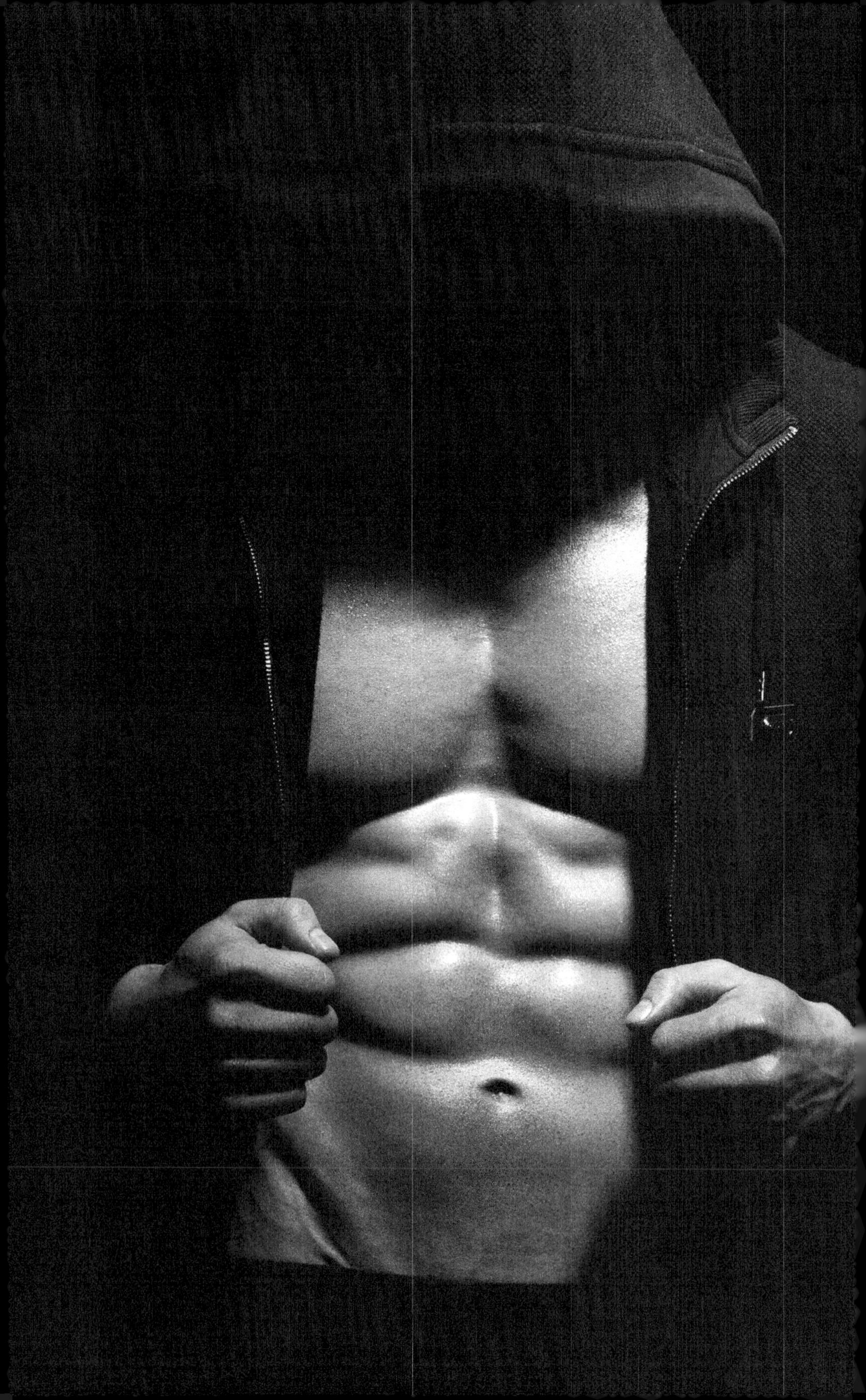

Chapter Seven

Jax

I couldn't even begin to tell you how powerful last night was. I've been with my fair share of women, but nothing had ever felt like that. Piper's touch was explosive, addictive and I wanted more.

I couldn't get my head around why she was so insecure about herself, she was an absolute smoke show. The most stunning woman I'd ever encountered. Not only was she simply beautiful and I of course wanted more of her body, but I was overtaken with the urge to get to know her better. I'd never felt that way with anybody. Everybody always just saw me as a good time, you know, stripper Jax is always up for a good time. I was, to an extent. But there was much more to me than that and I had the feeling that Piper would be the one to uncover it. She didn't just care about the outside package, she seemed to actually like ... me.

We exchanged numbers last night before we parted ways and I was grateful, there was no way that one evening with her would be enough. I wanted more, so I sent the text that had been rattling around in my brain since I woke up this morning.

> **Me:** Hi Blondie, I just wanted to send you a message to thank you for last night. It was … amazing. I'd really like to see you again, if you'd like to of course? Jax x

I felt like a teenage boy sending his crush a text for the very first time. I waited and waited for Piper's reply, finally after what felt like an eternity but was probably closer to five minutes, the three little dots appeared,

> **Blondie:** Hi Jax. Last night … wow! Last night was one of the best nights of my life, I'd love to see you again. If you're sure? P x

There she goes again, I just had to get to the bottom of that insecurity and what was causing it.

> **Me:** I'd like nothing more, I'm working every evening for the rest of the week but how about a breakfast date? Louie's does a lovely brekkie if you fancy it? Jax x

I still hadn't had the chance to talk to Louie about him retiring, now was that chance. There was no way I'd let that slip through my fingers, I already had enough to put a deposit down if he would accept it.

> **Blondie:** Breakfast sounds perfect. How about tomorrow? I have to drop my daughter off at school at 8:45am but I can meet you around 9:00am? P x

> **Me:** That sounds perfect Pipes, I'll meet you at Louie's in the morning then. Looking forward to it already. Have a great day beautiful. Jax x

Don't even ask me where these nicknames were coming from. I'd never been a nickname kind of dude, but Piper was bringing something out in me. It was insane really, I'd known her for not even twenty four hours yet. Maybe I was having some sort of quarter life crisis from my emotionally stunted youth. Who knows.

The day flew by and before I knew it, I was back in my dressing room smearing oil all over my chest and abs. Piper and our breakfast date had been on my mind all day, I couldn't get the woman out of my mind. That curvy body, those lush lips, her sweet coconut scent and that laugh. Wow, I'd never had such a visceral reaction to a laugh before. It make my chest warm and now I was hard.

    I usually got hard at work, dancing around with my clothes off while women practically threw themselves at my feet, usually got me going. But tonight, there was only one woman taking up every second in my thoughts and it was her that I was hard for. I'd have to take care of myself when I got off stage, usually I'd welcome a helping hand or even two, but tonight I wasn't interested.

    Mike called through with my two minute warning, I readjusted my hard cock in my boxers with a groan. I'd do anything to sink back into Piper's warm heat tonight, I'd just have to stick to my right hand. I'd completely freak her out if I text her for a booty call, that wasn't what she was at all but these new and fast feelings were even freaking me out. I don't know what had come over me.

    So, off I went to the stage and spent the next twenty minutes doing my thing. Grinding, thrusting, clenching my muscles, sweat pouring down my body. My body was there, my mind was not. I couldn't stop myself from looking for Piper in the audience. I knew she wasn't there of course. I was being completely ridiculous.

    I'd barely walked back through my dressing room door after my set, before lowing my boxers to my ankles and taking my hard cock in my hand. I turned and leaned my forehead against my closed dressing room door. Moving my hand fast and firm up and down my hard length. Blonde hair and blue eyes flashed behind my eyelids, aa I fucked into my own hand.

    My heart was racing, my pulse thrumming through my body. I was in my Piper fantasy land when a soft knock sounded at the door and a voice I knew too well sounded through the door.

"Jaxy, do you need a hand?," it was Shan, she was a regular here at the club. Although she wasn't necessarily a paying customer, she had given herself the job title of 'helping hand'. She was eager to please all of the male dancers who needed a little 'relief' after their performances. I couldn't think of anything worse in this moment.

"Not tonight Shan," I croaked through the door. She was killing my buzz. I heard footsteps move down the hallway before she was knocking on Danny's door next to mine, the same offer leaving her lips. Christ the woman had no shame.

I continued with my pumping, my eyes closed and my hips grinding into my fist. It didn't take long at all for me to be groaning out Piper's name and spurting come all over the wooden door. Hmm, that would take some explaining to the cleaning ladies later.

I couldn't help chuckling to myself before going off to find a baby wipe.

> Me: Goodnight Pipes, I was thinking of you tonight when I danced for all those women. Jax x

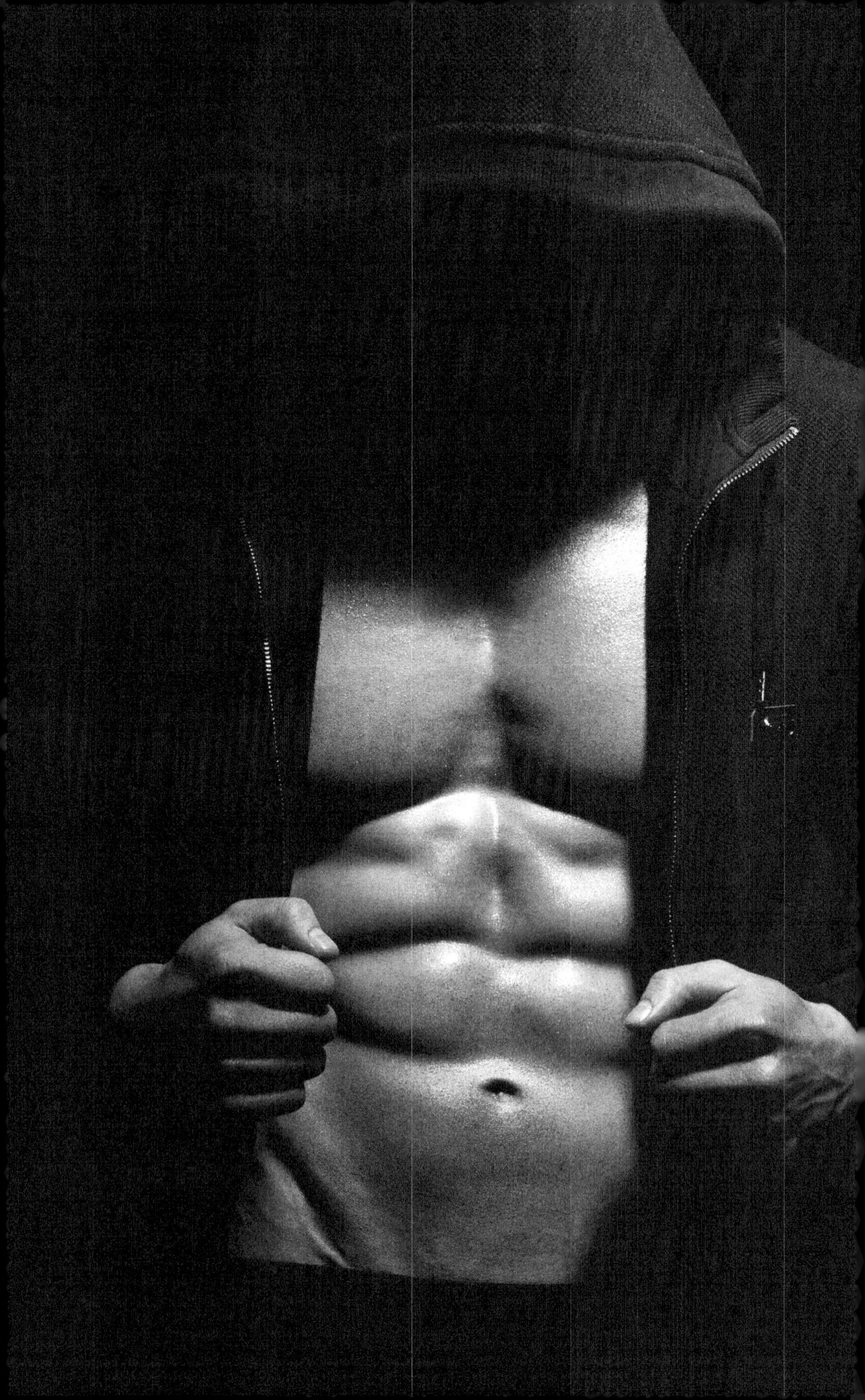

Chapter Eight

Piper

   Jax's honesty was refreshing. There was no reason for him to be so forward with me, we hardly knew each other. But I liked it, there was no messing around, no second guessing his thoughts and feelings. He was open and honest about everything. I had never been with a man like that before.
   When I received his text message last night telling me that he had been thinking of me, it made my heart pump in my chest and butterflies flood my tummy. I hadn't even admitted to myself that I was jealous of all of those women watching him, getting turned on by him. But something deep inside was feeling a little possessive.
   He was in no way 'mine'. He was eleven years younger than me for God sake, he could never truly be mine. He was only young, he had a lot of living left to do yet. But I was damn sure going to soak up every second of that mans attention, before he got bored with me and moved on to someone young and hot.

I'd just dropped Posie off at school and was now on my way to Louie's, I was a little nervous. My skin was buzzing with nerves, my pulse racing. I'd never been truly excited by a man before, until now.

I pulled open the heavy door to Louie's and saw him immediately. He was sat at the bar chatting with Louie, a huge smile plastered across his gorgeous face as he stood and shook his hand after handing the old man a cheque. I wondered what that was about. I didn't have to wait long to find out before Jax spun around and spotted me instantly. He came bounding over like an excited golden retriever, took me in his huge muscled arms and span me around.

"I did it Pipes, I really did it!", he exclaimed excitedly.

I couldn't help but giggle as I held on for dear life, my little arms stretched around his big shoulders.

"What did you do?", I managed to breath out as he squeezed me tightly.

"Oh shit, sorry," he immediately placed my feet back down on the floor and held me by the shoulders.

"Are you ok? I didn't mean to be so rough, I just got a little overexcited", he stroked his thumb down my cheek and across my bottom lip before leaning in and ghosting his soft lips over mine. All conversation was soon forgotten as we got caught up in the moment. He hauled me into his chest before devouring my mouth with his, a deep groan leaving his throat. It felt like a public claiming and I was here for it.

Jax eventually pulled back and looked down into my eyes, his hooded greens full of lust.

"Shit, sorry again," he huffed out a laugh before rubbing

the back of his neck with one hand. The action caused his big bicep to bulge and stretch against his white t-shirt. This man was delicious.

"It's fine", I whispered as I lowered my face to his warm neck. He smelt like man, mint and soap, "I thoroughly enjoyed that". I peeked up and gave him a shy smile. He huffed out a breath of relief before taking my hand and leading me towards our table. He didn't sit opposite me, but shuffled in next to me on the bench, taking my hand in his and resting it in his lap.

"I enjoyed it too baby, I've wanted to do that again since the second we left each other the other night".

"Really?," I asked in disbelief.

"Oh hell yeah baby, if it wasn't completely inappropriate and we wouldn't get arrested then I'd totally bend you over this table right now", he whispered into my ear. Sending goose bumps to pebble across my flesh and wetness to my core.

"Hmm, I'd like that". I'd never been to brazen, so honest about what I wanted. It was a relief.

"All good things come to those who wait baby, or as I like to say, all good girls get to come if they just wait". He told me with a wink.

Holy crap, now my panties were soaked and I could feel my pulse thumping between my legs. I stared at him with wide eyes, a shy smile spreading across my face. I could feel the flush spread from my neck to my cheeks as I told him,

"I'm pretty good at waiting ...".

It was his turn to groan and shift uncomfortably in his seat, I lowered my eyes down his body and sucked in a surprised breath when I saw his hard dick tenting his grey joggers. Grey joggers and backwards hats should be illegal, am I right? Jax should be carted off to prison right this second. He was wearing a tight white tee, light grey joggers, pristine white trainers and a navy blue hat ... backwards.

I shook my head to dispel my naughty thoughts before eventually getting back to our previous conversation,

"What are you so excited about? Oh holy hell, not that excited! I didn't mean what made your ...", I pointed down to his crotch before slamming my forehead against my palm and shaking with laughter.

"I didn't mean why is your ... dick excited," I huffed a laugh, "I meant, what were you so excited about when I got here?".

Jax just stared at me, amusement in his eyes, a smirk pulling at his lips.

"I know what you meant ...". He chuckled, it was a beautiful sound that went on for a while. Before he opened up and told me all about his plans for the future. He briefly told me about his parents being addicts, he told me about his dream of owning a pub, not so much for the selling booze part. But, he wanted to be a listening ear to people who needed help.

I hadn't known this man long but I could already see how huge his heart was. He was sweet, funny, sexy, honest and so damn caring. We had a wonderful breakfast together, he held me tightly in his arms as he gave me a soft kiss goodbye.

"Goodbye ... for now baby". He told me with a wink, it felt like the most delicious promise anyone had ever made me.

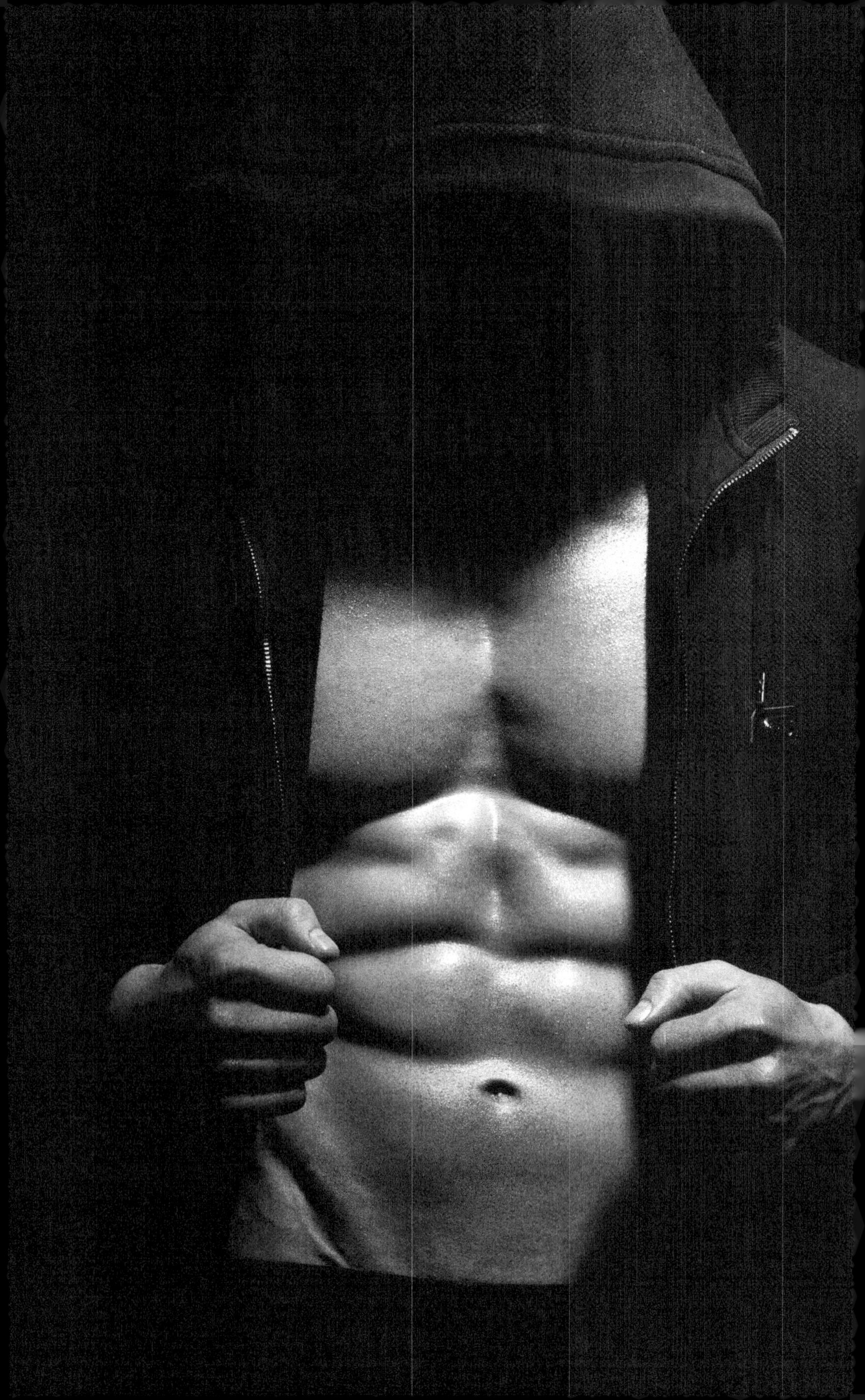

Chapter Nine

Jax

Me: Hi :D x

Blondie: Hey you x

Me: What are you wearing? x

Blondie: Ha, actually nothing at the moment. Just got out of the bath x

    I couldn't hold back the groan that left my throat, this woman was killing me.

> Me: Pipes, you can't tell me that. Now I'm hard at work, might have to knock one out again like the other night. Thinking of you obviously! x

> Blondie: You … took care of business the other night? Because of me? x

This woman had absolutely no idea how fucking sexy she was.

> Me: You want me to tell you about it? x

> Blondie: Hell yes! x

> Me: Well I'd just finished my set onstage, which I'd spent the entire time thinking about you and wishing you were in the audience again. By the time I got back to my room, I was so hard it was painful Pipes. I needed you baby. I was offered a helping hand but I just wanted you x

> Blondie: You turned down another woman because you wanted me? x

> Me: Hell yeah I did. Things are intense between us baby. Please tell me you feel it too? x

I'd always been pretty good at opening up and sharing my feelings, I didn't see the point in keeping those kind of things inside. Ace was always taking the piss out of me, telling me that I'm like a huge puppy dog. I'll take it, dogs are cute right?

> **Blondie: ...**

> **Blondie: I feel it too Jax. Insane though don't you think? We haven't known each other long x**

It was insane ... insanely fucking brilliant! My entire adult life so far I've felt like I was searching for something. I think that's probably why I've never had a serious relationship. Nothing ever felt right, it always just felt shallow. A quick fuck to take the edge off.

> **Me: It is pretty fast baby but I'm not fighting it. I'm not scared x**

> **Blondie: I'm glad one of us isn't because I'm terrified. What happened the other night? After you turned down help x**

Hmm, dirty girl wanted details. I couldn't help myself when I reached inside my joggers and wrapped my hand around my already hard cock, using my thumb to swipe at the moisture beading around my piercing.

> **Me: Well baby, I was so hard it hurt. I wrapped my hand around my hard cock, leaned my head against my door and stroked myself. Hard and**

> **fast, imagining it was your hand … x**

I tugged on my cock with one hand, still texting Piper with the other. My skin pebbled with pleasure, tiny beads of sweat skating down my spine. I could picture her right now, wrapped in her towel fresh from the bath. Laying on her back on her bed, legs spread wide whilst teasing her clit with her fingers. My cock grew impossibly harder.

> **Me: Are you touching yourself Pipes? x**

> **Blondie: Yes! Keep going x**

> **Me: I grasped my dick hard, moving my hand up and down. Feeling all the grooves and ridges. I imagined you were on your knees in front of me Pipes, swallowing down every drop as I came hard. So hard x**

> **Blondie: I'm so wet Jax, I'm so close x**

This was so far out of Piper's comfort zone but she was owning it, owning her pleasure, with me. I was so damn proud of her.

> **Me: I'm gonna come baby, open wide x**

I closed my eyes tight as I came so hard all over my hands and abs, I was totally spent. An idea flashed in my mind and before I could stop myself I snapped a picture of the mess I'd made. I took a few seconds to consider what I was doing and went for it anyway.

> **Me: It was all for you baby. [Image of come covered abs and cock] x**

> **Blondie: Holy shit x**

Piper was silent for a few minutes, I could only imagine what had happened and my God, I would do anything to be right there with her! A few seconds later, a picture came through and my heart just about stopped.

> **Blondie: [Image of come covered fingers}**

Shit. I swiped a hand down my face as I tried to regain my composure.

> **Me: That was the hottest picture I've ever seen in my life Blondie. I'm so proud of you, you sexy woman! x**

I literally had a few minutes before I had to take to the stage, somehow I just wasn't feeling it anymore. My cock was soft, I felt relaxed, satiated. This was going to be a hard set to get through.

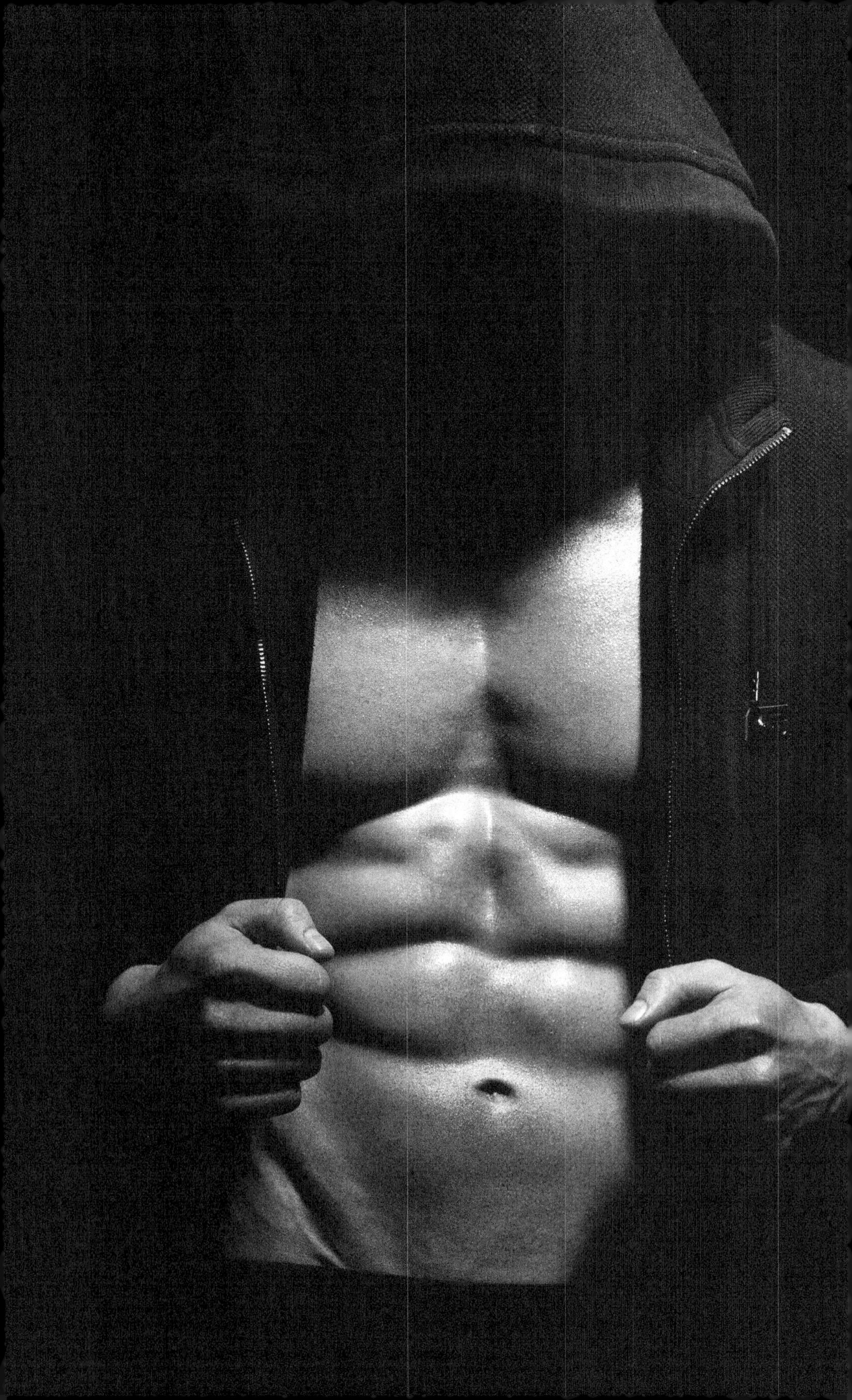

Chapter Ten

Piper

March

> Jax: What's your favourite colour? x

> Me: Emerald Green ... like your eyes x

April

> Jax: Happy Easter! Check your door step, the Easter bunny left something for you and Posie x

Me: Jax, has anyone ever told you what a sweetheart you are? Posie loved her Easter basket full of goodies, thank you x

May

Me: I think it's time ... I'd really love for you to meet Posie. Want to come to dinner when you next have a night off work? x

Jax: I'd love to. Nothing would make me happier x

Me: Thank you for being so sweet with Posie. She loves you ... x

Jax: I loved her too. I'm also pretty fond of her Mum x

I'd known Jax for four months now and it was pretty safe to say that I'd fallen in love with him. He was everything I'd ever hoped for in a partner. He was sweet and loyal, kind and caring and he built me up like nobody else had ever done.

Posie loved him just as much as I did, we spent every free second together. Posie spent most weekends at her Dad's house which left them free for me to soak up every second with Jax. He was unfortunately working tonight though, he was so close to his target for opening up his pub. He put a down payment on it a few months ago. Louie was planning to retire by the end of month, which gave Jax around two weeks left at the club.

I would always have a special place in my heart for that club, it was where I met Jax. But the stronger my feelings grew for him, the harder it was to accept his job. I didn't like that he was showing his body to countless women and men every night. I was jealous and I wasn't afraid to admit it.

I knew that Jax had feelings for me too, we hadn't said those three little words to each other yet but I didn't really feel like we had to. Jax showed me that he loved me every single day, with his actions and his words. It would be nice to hear it though.

He made me love myself, I no longer had the huge body image issues that I had only a few months ago. Now, don't get me wrong, there are still moments when I look at myself in the mirror and don't like what I see. But I've come to learn that it's ok, we can't love ourselves completely one hundred percent of the time. That's unachievable. However, like my very wise boyfriend tells me "It's ok not to love every part of yourself all of the time, because when you don't, I will".

He made me feel so loved, desired. My confidence had grown massively since we met and I couldn't be more grateful to him. That's why I was here, on a Saturday night, hiding away in Jax's dressing room whilst he was out on stage.

He had no idea I was here. He quite often told me that he was always incredibly turned on by the time he came back in here. I'd even heard about the woman that offered the guys some 'help'. I was sick of her offering it to Jax so I was here to stake my claim and I didn't care what anyone else thought about it.

Jax was due off stage any minute, so here I was checking myself out in his floor length mirror. I was wearing all white, a tiny lace thong and matching bra. Sky high heels that made my arse look great. My hair was in thick waves around my shoulders and I had on my pink lipstick that Jax wasn't shy about telling me he likes.

The longer I looked in that mirror, the more I started to question what I was doing, what I was wearing. Would Jax like what he saw, or would he secretly be wishing for a younger, fitter model.

I didn't have much time to second guess myself before I heard shuffling in the hallway, the door to Jax's dressing room swung open and in he strode. He hadn't noticed me yet, he was too busy pulling his boxer briefs below his arse and taking out his hard cock that had been straining against them.

His eyes were closed, his back leaning against the closed door, oh shit, what if he was expecting someone? What if he said another woman's name? I slunk quietly backwards into the corner of the room, he still hadn't opened his eyes and noticed me standing here.

He was moving his hand up and down his hard length frantically, his chest heaving and his breaths coming quickly.

"Mmm Pipes", he murmured. It was a shot to my heart, thank fuck for that, he was thinking about me.

That's what put my next movements into action. I slowly sashayed away from the corner of the room, my heels silent on the carpeted floor. Before I reached for him, I took account of his strained facial expression. His abs contracted with every flex of his hand against himself.

I moved up close, he still hadn't noticed me, he was too engrossed in getting himself off. As I moved closer, I could smell him. Sweaty, musky, man and with a hint of aftershave. He smelt divine as I lowered myself to my knees in front of him and reached to stroke my fingertips up his inner thigh.

He jumped a foot in the air and moved ever closer to the door as his eyes flew open and locked on mine. The shocked expression on his face very quickly changed to a potent lust. His green eyes caressed every single inch of my body.

My pulse was racing as I squeezed my thighs together in an attempt to ease the ache which was building.

He reached for me with two hands, me still on my knees in front of him. He rested his giant paws on either side of my face and pulled me to him.

"Come here baby, ease the ache".

He grabbed the base of his cock with one hand and swiped the tip across my bottom lip. I immediately opened for him, caressing him with my tongue and licking up the come that was already leaking from him.

"Take it all baby", he was barely restraining himself before I took him as deep as I could. He hit the back of my throat repeatedly as I took him faster and faster. Both of his hands were clutching the roots of my hair as he thrust his hips into my waiting mouth. His muscled abs were glistening, contracting with every pulse.

I couldn't help but rub my thighs together and grind down on the heel of my foot, desperate to ease the throb.

In a flash, Jax pulled his dripping cock from my mouth and heaved me up onto my feet. He wrapped his giant arms around my body and lifted me from the floor. I instantly wrapped my legs around his tight waist as he carried me to the sofa in the middle of the room.

He settled back, taking me onto his lap.

"I need inside you Pipes, if I'm going to finish anywhere, I want it to be deep inside of you".

He stroked his giant hands down my back, reaching the tiny string that was nestled between my arse cheeks. He pulled it tight before swiping his thick fingers down my crack. Digging his fingers into my arse cheeks before placing a hand on each of my hips and pulling me down to grind on his hard length. He was rock solid, like a steel pipe between his legs.

He pushed a finger into the side of my panties, pulling them away from my body and unveiling my dripping core to the room. He swiped one knuckle through my wetness before positioning his cock at my entrance and lowering me onto him in one, smooth thrust.

I began to ride him, faster and faster. We were both right on the precipice of a monster orgasm. At that moment, a soft knock sounded at the door and a quiet voice snaked through the wood,

"Jaxy, do you need a hand?". I knew who this woman was instantly. I looked down into Jax's relaxed, hooded eyes. He opened his mouth to answer her, before I slammed a hand down over his lips and called out.

"Jax will never need a helping hand again, he's mine". Those words caused Jax to grab my hips and pound up into me relentlessly. I couldn't stop the loud moan that left my lips as I came so hard I almost blacked out.

Thrust, thrust, thrust.

Jax stilled, growing impossibly harder inside of me. He looked deep into my eyes before coming violently with a shout,

"I'm hers! I'm hers! And she's fucking mine", he growled the last word as he continued to pump into me slowly before crashing his lips to mine.

We sat quietly for long moments, catching out breath. I was still perched in his lap, his fingertips stroking up and down my spine. Goose bumps pebbled across my body, his warm breath against my neck as he spoke the most beautiful words I'd ever heard.

"Piper baby. Blondie, I'm so deeply in love with you. You own my heart, you own my soul, you own my forever ...".

A silent tear left my eye and trickled down my cheek. The happiest tear that's every been.

"I love you too baby, you've changed my life. I'm keeping you forever".

He pulled my lips down to his for the most beautiful kiss of my life, full of love, full of promises.

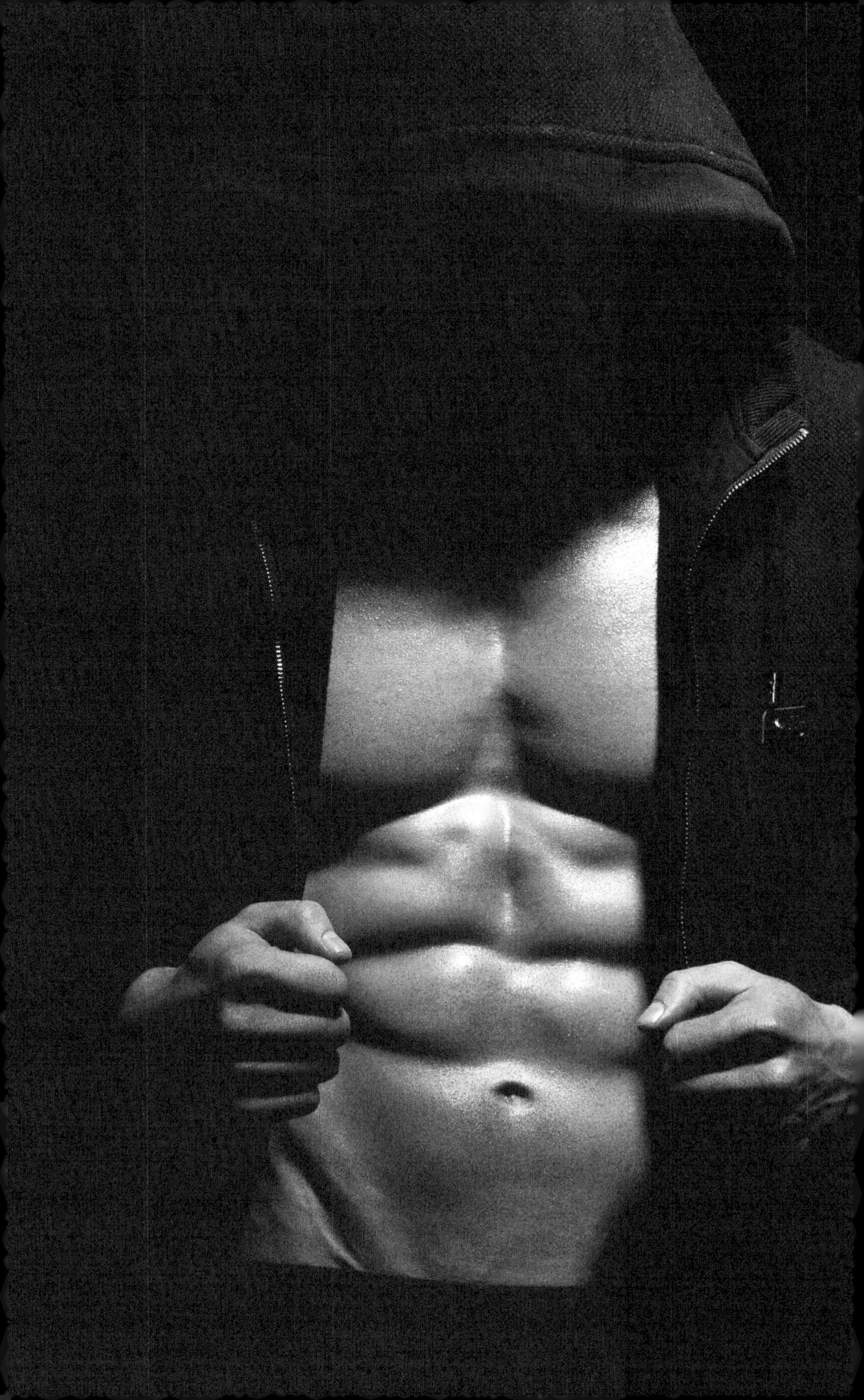

Chapter Eleven

Jax

It had been a long time since anyone had told me that they loved me, in fact the last and only person who had ever said those words to me was my brother Ace. Our childhood had been incredibly fucked up, our parents had been addicts for as long as I can remember.

We spent our days living in filth, eating old food from the fridge because there was rarely anything fresh. We were dirty, skinny little kids. It was a miracle that we made it to adulthood to be completely honest with you.

I'd never forget a single detail about those days, we woke up together on a piss stained mattress. No blankets, no pillows. We huddled together for body heat. Ace was three years older than me and for as long as I can remember, he was my protector. My hero. We rarely had any food in so it wasn't often that we had breakfast before going to school, any food we did have was stolen from the corner shop down the road. I truly believe that the owners knew what we were doing whenever we went in there, but we never got into trouble. They turned a blind eye to the two little smelly kids stealing from them. If they hadn't, we would have starved.

Mum and Dad were constantly being called into school, questioned about our wellbeing and the bruises that littered our little bodies. They had it all so well rehearsed though that they managed to get out of it every single time. Looking back now, I wish we would have had the courage to speak up and tell the truth, the trouble was that when you were constantly threatened with a whipping from Dad's belt, we were easily silenced.

That's what happened at home, whether we were good little boys or not. When Dad got back from the pub or whatever whore he'd spent the day with, that's when he came to spend time with us. Ace always tried to take my beatings, the ones that I 'deserved', but Dad quickly caught on to the fact that he was trying to protect me. That made things even worse, he loved to watch Ace losing his shit whilst he pounded on me. He got some sort of sick pleasure out of watching his little boys hurting because of him.

Dad was power hungry and an absolute bastard.

If he wasn't beating on us then he was beating and raping our mother, while we were forced to watch. It got to the point where we were numb to it, we had been forced to watch so many times that it didn't hurt us anymore. Our mother wasn't a mother, she was a shell of a woman who whored herself out to pay for Dad's habit.

As an adult, I see now that she was a victim too. He hurt her just like he hurt us. She couldn't find a way out, but she didn't even try. She sat at the kitchen table, smoking cigarette after cigarette whilst watching her children getting beaten half to death. What kind of parent did that.

I remember so vividly one day in particular. I must have been around six, Ace was nine. We had just come in from school, stolen food hidden in the bottom of our backpacks.

We tiptoed through the house, not that there was any need to be quiet, the music in here was deafening. That only meant one thing, Mum and Dad had 'company'. We made it half way up the stairs to our bedroom when Dad came flying out of the kitchen and pounded up the stairs behind us. There was no point in trying to run, it would only make it worse. He grabbed each of us by the collar and dragged us back down towards the kitchen,

"Come and look at this boys", he said with a demented sneer plastered across his face. I hated this man with every fibre of my being. I'd already made a pact with myself that one day, when I was old enough, I'd kill him. It would be my turn to protect Ace and repay him for all the beatings he took on my behalf.

Dad dragged us into the kitchen and I couldn't even begin to describe the scene in front of me. Six and nine year old little boys should never see what we saw that day. Our mother was tied to the dining room table, arms and legs tightly secured to the table legs. She was naked, covered in blood and bruises. In the room with her were six men, seven including Dad. They all stood with their cocks out. That enough would have been completely inappropriate for a child to see, but nope. They were taking turns raping my mother. She was unconscious, I remember thinking that she must have taken lots of those white pills to be sleeping through all of that trauma. But no, I later found out that my mother was dead.

She must have had prior warning of Dad's evening plans for her, she overdosed before they arrived and she died on that table. She took her last breath while countless men were abusing her and her husband stood by and watched. She left us a note that we found later on that night, when we had been allowed to leave the kitchen.

> Boys, there's nothing I can say apart from I'm sorry. I

> wasn't good enough, I wasn't strong enough. Goodbye.

No I love you's, no I regret not protecting you. Nope, she took a bunch of pills and left us. Not that she protected us anyway, but with Mum gone. Dad turned all of his attention on to us boys.

We endured years and years of torture from that man, he starved us, he beat us, he neglected us. He put us in the hospital more times than I could count, he always had a convincing story to back himself up with though, so managed to stay out of trouble. The only good days were when he disappeared for weeks on end and forgot all about us.

It wasn't until we got bigger, when I was around twelve and Ace fifteen that we got big enough to fight back. We didn't fight back often though because we knew that it would just make Dad extra cruel the next time.

Things came to an abrupt end a few years later when Ace turned eighteen, something in him snapped that day. Ace came home from working at the local fast food restaurant. He hadn't had the job long as he had been too worried to leave me alone with Dad. But we needed the money, we were bigger now. Stealing pieces of fruit from the corner shop wasn't going to cut it anymore.

Anyway, Ace came home to find me in the same position we had found our mother in all those years ago. The only difference was that there wasn't half a dozen men in there with me. No, just Dad, with his belt. He had hit me hard enough to knock me out, stripped me butt naked and strapped me down on that table. I woke up to him whipping me, relentless lashes of that belt swept across my burning skin. He whipped my chest, my legs, my arms. He even whipped me down there, I couldn't even begin to describe that pain and I'd never ever forget it either.

Ace walked in to find me bleeding, everywhere. Cuts and

lacerations littered my entire body, he'd even cut my dick open with the metal buckle on his belt. That was the day that Ace lost it, he beat my father to within an inch of his life. The only reason he stopped was because I couldn't lose my brother too, I couldn't survive in a world when he wasn't right here next to me. I couldn't watch him go down for murder, so I pleaded with him. I begged him from my table of pain, blood dripping from the table and pooling onto the floor. The world was going hazy and beginning to go dark around the edges.

Ace called an ambulance and they got there just in time, they managed to save my life. That day changed us both, we grew from boys to men in an instant. Dad was carted off to prison, charged with hundreds of counts of child abuse, torture, neglect. Luckily, Ace and I had kept a diary of the attacks since we were old enough to write. We had three boxes of journals stashed underneath the floorboards. Seeing those three boxes carted off by police was insane. They detailed our entire childhood. Every punch, every cigarette burn, every time we were thrown down the stairs. They also included a very detailed account of our mothers murder.

That was the last day we saw our Dad, in court as we stood up in front of him and sent him to prison for life. Unbelievably, that moment meant nothing to me. I was numb, I didn't care that we didn't have parents anymore. We didn't have them in the first place. It didn't affect me at all. Until we left that court room and Ace pulled me into his arms. He was big and strong, muscled now that he was a man. He held me and he told me that he loved me. He'd said it countless times over the years, when he was nursing my wounds or holding me on that piss stained mattress. But when he told me that day, I realised that as long as I had my brother then I was going to be alright.

I grew up feeling like a worthless human being, my entire childhood I was told what a waste of space I was. Growing up in the house that we grew up in was a lonely business. Fighting for our lives everyday, fighting to not grow up like them when that could have been easily done. We had enough memories trapped inside our minds to warrant wanting to block it all out and numb it with drugs and alcohol. But it was something that we both refused to do, if I hadn't have had Ace then I would have ended up in the same pit of despair as they did. Ace brought me up, Ace taught me right from wrong and Ace is the reason I'm the decent human being I am today.

People were always commenting on my happy go lucky nature, my flirty banter, my confidence. I learnt that from my brother, when you've been at rock bottom you appreciate what it means to be free. Free from torture, free from pain, free from numbness and despair. You grow to appreciate the little things and the good people in life.

My brother loved me and now Piper loved me, what a lucky son of a bitch I was.

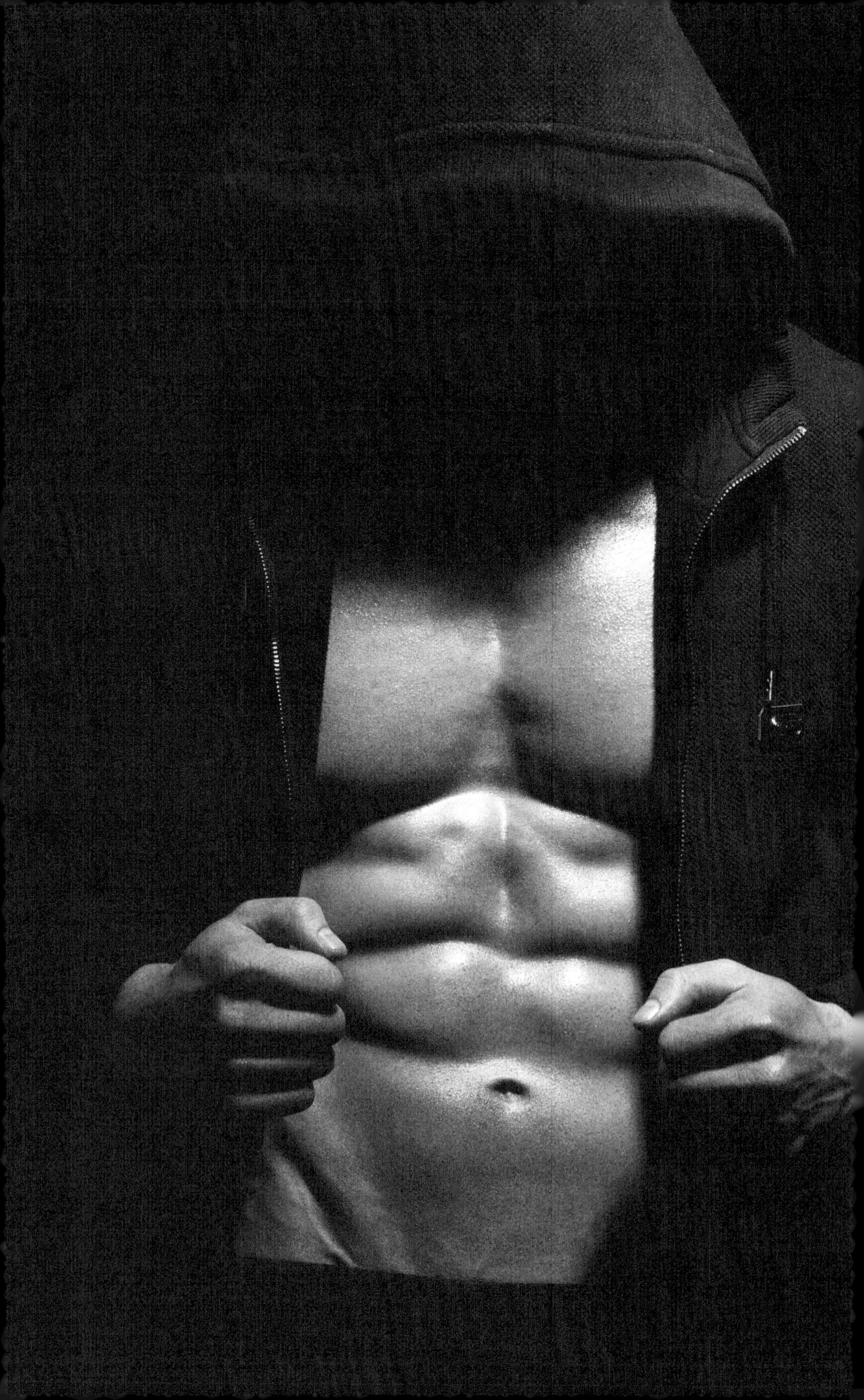

Chapter Twelve

Jax

I had one week left working at the club and then I was a free man. I was signing the mortgage for the pub today and I was on top of the world. The pub included a three bedroom flat which was on the upper level and that would be my home too. I hadn't asked her yet but I had my heart set on Piper and Posie coming to live there with me too.

But first, it was mortgage time. Ace was picking me up and we were going together. We did all the big things together, we were partners. I heard him before I saw him, like usual. Now bear in mind that my brother is twenty-eight years old, he works as a firefighter and is a well respected member of the community. So when you hear 'Sweet Caroline' blaring out of his speakers, him singing along, all whilst rolling up in his self proclaimed 'Nosh Wagon', you can't help but laugh. My brother was a fuck boy, the biggest fuck boy I'd ever met. He was always completely honest and upfront about that fact and of course, always treated women with respect. He just went through a lot of them. And enjoyed them in his car most of the time, hence the name 'Nosh Wagon'.

I gingerly opened the door, climbing inside whilst making it very obvious that I was checking for bodily fluids before I sat down.

"There he is, the man of the hour!" He shouted over his music, thumping me on the back with his giant hand. He was a big guy, a couple of inches taller than me, dark brown hair which always looked like he'd been dragged through a bush backwards. He was big and broad, muscled, tattooed. But was honestly such a massive softie that his appearance was a total contradiction to his character. This man would do absolutely anything for anybody, he loved me and his friends fiercely.

I knew better though, like with me, the persona was a little bit of a cover up. Yes he was beyond confident, his self esteem was through the roof and he was always laughing and joking. But deep down, under all of those layers was a broken little boy fucked up by his parents. Ace had a massive fear of losing people, he held his friends so close to his heart, they were the family we never had. When one of them was hurting then so was he, he was sensitive and emotional, but managed to cover it up with a thick layer of banter most of the time.

Like for example, Ace's best buddy Hugh and his wife Grace are expecting a baby in November. I'm pretty sure Ace is more nervous than the expectant parents, he holds an inability to settle and let things go. He worries and he stresses, he spends too much time considering all the 'what ifs' that sometimes he forgets to just live in the moment and enjoy life. I think that's probably one of the main reasons why he hasn't tried to settle down with anybody, he doesn't trust anybody not to hurt him. He doesn't trust that he could give his heart to somebody and they wouldn't break it. I hope he finds somebody one day, he has a big heart and I'd love to see him settled and happy with the right person.

I dread the day he gets his heart broken though, it will probably happen one day and I know for a fact that he won't deal well with it.

"I'm here, I'm here. Let's get this show on the road and go and buy a pub!". I was so excited to finally be starting my dream. I had the woman, I had her little girl and now I'd have my very own home with my very own pub underneath.

Papers were signed, contracts were exchanged and now the final wait was underway. Louie was moving out this weekend and I'd be moving in next weekend. The pub was going to be closed for the next few weeks whilst it underwent some work. It was perfectly fine as it was but I wanted to put my own stamp on things. Ace and Hugh had both taken time off work for the next ten days to help me out, we were doing most of the work ourselves. Ryan and Mack were going to come along and help us in the evenings, I'd heard Mack was a dab hand with a chainsaw which unfortunately we didn't have a current need for. But he was bringing his table saw along and was making me some custom tables and a custom bar.

I'd spent a very long time dreaming up my perfect pub, I'd managed to save up a lot of money, mostly from my tips at the club. I planned on putting every single penny to good use. I wanted it to be absolutely perfect.

I was going to miss the club, for years it had become a place to let loose and leave my worries at the door. It had done the world of good for my self confidence and I'd made some good friends there. They were all planning on coming along to the pub opening, even though they were in the next town over, they were coming to support me. Mike was the first to put his name down and reserve a table. That man had seen things no security guy should ever see, he'd found me in many a precarious position back in my fuckboy days. But he somehow managed to look past the memory of my naked arse, cock and balls and become my friend anyway. The poor guy was twice my age, dealt with randy fuckers night after night and still managed to have a smile on his face for me.

  I couldn't wait to show everybody what I was made of, I wasn't just a pretty face and a shallow guy who just took his clothes off for a few quid here and there. There was much more to me than that and I couldn't wait to prove it to everybody. First though, I had my last week at the club to look forward to. The guys had planned a bit of a send off for me on Friday night, I had no idea what to expect but I knew for sure that I was looking forward to it.

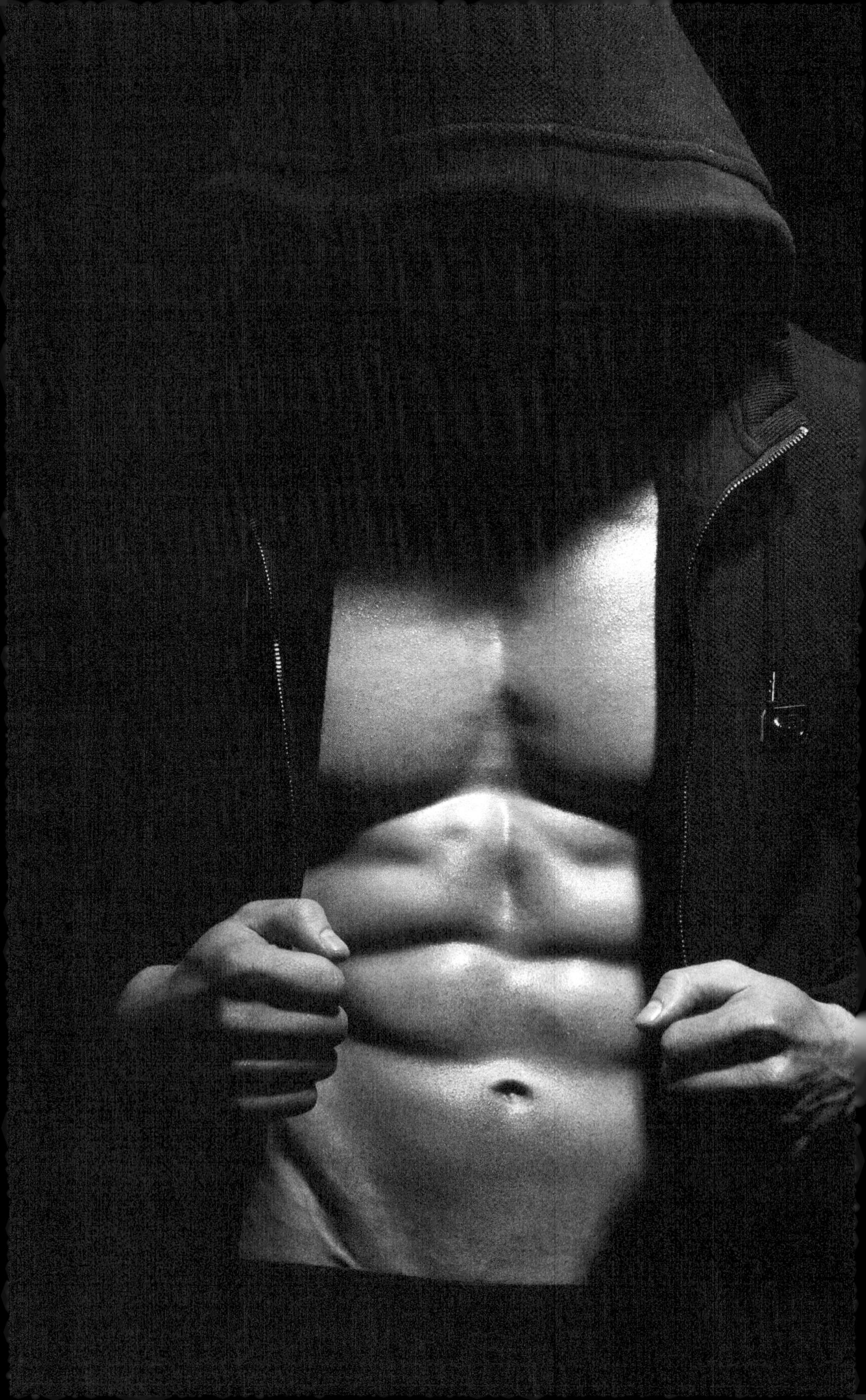

Chapter Thirteen

Piper

It had been a busy week at the surgery, pet owners came in for all manner of reasons. Some were normal, legit reasons to bring your animal to the vet. Some reasons were absolutely ludicrous and were hard to get your head around. Like the vibrating four year old cocker spaniel who was brought in for swallowing poor Mrs Finley's nine inch vibrator ... whole! Hardly chewed the thing! Maisie and I were in fits of giggles as we prepped poor Misty for her operation to remove it, there was no way that was coming out the usual way.

"Damn, the doggy deep throated goooooood", Maisie fell about laughing. Hands on her knees as she struggled to rein herself in. It was looking at the x ray that had set her off, there it was in all its glory. Lodged deep inside the poor dogs stomach, there was something else in there too which was unrecognisable. Hopefully we could figure things out when we got in there.

Forty minutes later, the giant dildo had been retrieved

along with six unopened condoms, a butt plug and a small vibrating egg ... which was still vibrating. The poor dog must have been so uncomfortable and poor Mrs Finley turned the colour of a ripe tomato when we showed her what we'd found.

   It was safe to say that I loved my job, I saw some weird and wonderful things and I loved doing it all with Maisie by my side. She was a force to be reckoned with and had managed to bag herself a gorgeous husband Mack. Maisie and Mack were both twenty seven and had been married for three years, they were complete opposites in every single way. Where Maisie was confident and outspoken, Mack was like a quiet little puppy dog. They were adorable together and he worshipped the ground she walked on. He was fiercely protective of her, which was why our plans for tonight could go one way or the other.

   It was Jax's last night at the club tonight and all his work buddies had thrown together a surprise for him, along with all his friends, his brother Ace and myself. Posie was spending an extra night with her Dad, which left me to enjoy the festivities. I was extremely nervous and had tried to talk myself out of it multiple times but Maisie was having none of it. I'd committed to it, along with Maisie. To be honest Maisie was only doing it to support me, she had come up with the insane idea when I spoke to her about not knowing what to do for Jax for his final night. I'd gone along with this idea because it had been weeks and weeks away. Now it wasn't, it was tonight and I was absolutely terrified.

It was nine pm on Friday night. It was Jax's very last night working at the club, he'd just come off stage himself and was in his changing room doing his thing and getting ready for his leaving do which was starting at ten. Little did he know that we were all already here, his friends were hiding out in the back room, drinking and laughing. Everybody was here, Hugh and Grace, Mack and Ace and some of Jax's other friends that I hadn't really met yet.

I was in one of the changing rooms. Maisie was by my side, primping herself in the floor length mirror. Fluffing up her gorgeous red hair and applying her lipstick. She was wearing a pair of tiny denim shorts and a red tartan shirt that showed off her smooth tanned tummy and tied between her breasts. Along with a pair of sky high black heels with bright red bottoms. She looked absolutely stunning. She looked tall and slim, had legs for days and made me feel like a child standing next to her.

I was wearing a tiny navy skirt with matching heels and a white shirt tied the same as Maisie's. My hair was in big loose curls around my shoulders and my make up was perfect, my eyes smoky and my lips in my signature pink. I stood in front of that mirror and couldn't help but scrutinise every single part of my body. I was at least six inches shorter than Maisie, even with my heels on. Where her body was tight and smooth, mine was bumpy and podgy. Her shirt perfectly showed off a toned midriff whilst I felt like an overfilled sausage with lumps and bumps and extra weight trying to burst over the top of my skirt. I knew I wasn't overweight, but I definitely didn't look anything like Maisie. Her breasts were perky and her cleavage was to die for. She was a perfect ten. And I was just ... me.

Maisie was humming along to the music playing, swaying her hips to the music as she sipped on her champagne and waited for our big moment.

"I can't do this", I whispered in a tiny voice as a tear dripped from my eye, leaving a streak through my foundation.

"Hmm?" Maisie asked, turning towards me with her perfect shiny smile. Her face instantly dropped when she saw my face and took me in. Her eyes moved around my face and down my body, her head resting to one side, appraising me with her eyes. Obviously looking for the problem.

"I can't do this Maisie", I offered again. My face crumpled and the tears began to flow freely.

"What do you mean you can't do this?" Maisie set down her champagne glass and was by my side in an instant, taking me in her arms and pulling me to her chest. She was such an outgoing, confident, outspoken woman. She reminded me a little bit of those overly confident girls you'd come up against in high school. You know the ones, the super popular girls who had all the boys after them. They always turned out to be super bitchy though and I could never quite get my head around how they were so popular.

Maisie reminded me of those girls, but without the nastiness. She was the biggest sweetheart and she would always stand up for her friends through thick and thin.

I tried to fight against the tears, my chest heaving as I tried to regain my control,

"Look at me Maisie", I gestured down my body with my hand. "Look at me and then look at you", the last word broke on a sob.

"Pipes come here". Maisie pulled me in front of her and turned me to look at myself in the mirror. It was a hard thing to do. When I felt so uncomfortable in my own skin and so completely out of my depth.

"Do you know what I see when I look at you?" Maisie asked softly, softer than I'd ever heard her speak.

"A big, fat mess?" I choked on a laugh, nothing about this was funny though.

"I see a truly beautiful human being, not just on the outside but on the inside too. But let's start with the outside shall we? Now, you are not going to say a word ok. You are to listen to me".

She gave me a stern look in the mirror, hands on her hips and waited for me to nod. She would be a great mother one day.

She reached up and ran her hands through my hair.

"Do you know what I'd do for hair like this? You look like damn Rapunzel. It's so soft and shiny and so blonde it's almost white. People pay a lot of damn money for that colour and you grew it all by yourself".

She moved her hand to my chin, using a finger to push it up so that I was looking at myself once again.

"You have the most beautiful blue eyes Pipes, the cutest button nose and perfect kissable lips. If I was attracted to women, I'd be all over you like a rash".

All I could manage was a tiny smile.

Next, she grabbed two handfuls of my boobs, no shame, no embarrassment, just grabbed them.

"Do you know what I'd do for a pair of knockers like these? Holy hell Pipes, you're just being greedy. Look at them, it's like you have a couple of damn grapefruits stuffed in your bra!".

I still said nothing, just looked at her in the mirror. I wanted to believe her, God I did. I'd spent much of my adult life being belittled and ignored by my ex husband, who had cheated on me throughout our marriage which obviously did nothing for my self esteem.

Maisie's hands were on the move again, grabbing a handful of my arse, she said nothing, just mimicked a chefs kiss in the mirror.

"These legs are to die for too Pipes. I know you're short but short is cute. Jax is massive and he loves that you're so much smaller than him. Do you know how difficult it can be for tall women? I'm taller than most men, that's really fucking hard.

I'm just lucky that I managed to get a giant to fall in love with me".

A quick nod is all she got.

"Lastly, this tummy", she rested her hands across my tummy, pulling me into her for a hug from behind.

"Do you know the best thing about this tummy?" She asked barely above a whisper.

I shook my head, remaining silent.

"You grew a human in here Pipes, a whole human. You gave somebody life. Do you know how unbelievable that is and how lucky you are? Some women have trouble with that Pipes, you're miraculous. You're perfect ...". Her voice cracked on the last word, with a furrowed brow I turned and took in the complete devastation in her eyes. She didn't need to verbalise, I knew.

"Oh Maisie, I had no idea, I'm so sorry". It was my turn to take her in my arms, which looked ridiculous with our height difference as she practically smothered me with her boobs.

"It's ok, It'll happen when it's supposed to happen", she swiped her tears, slapped on her sunshine smile and turned me back to the mirror.

"Enough of that", she announced. She didn't even give me the chance to say anything more, she just gave me a look that told me that it wasn't up for discussion. Not now, maybe not ever.

"Do you know what the best thing about you is Piper?". I shook my head, now feeling like I was being totally stupid and insensitive. Here I was complaining about my baby body when I was damn lucky to have had a child in the first place.

"You are the kindest, sweetest, most compassionate woman I've ever met. You take care of everybody and you're always there for anyone who needs you. You see past peoples flaws Pipes and see the real them. Not everybody wears their hearts on their sleeves Pipes, but you do. You don't judge a book by it's cover, you see the real them. The real person behind the mask and then you love them unconditionally, flaws and all. Look at Jax for example, that man has had a hard life. I don't know how much he's shared with you but I know he will in his own time. But do you know how many women have taken advantage of his good looks and cheeky attitude? How many people have looked at him and only seen 'Jax The Stripper' and come to all sorts of disgusting conclusions? You see the real man, the man beneath the mask and I've never ever seen him happier and more content than he is now. Beneath the surface is a tender and scared little boy, who just wants to be loved. You complete him Pipes, in every single way possible and don't you ever forget it".

She blew my mind. I wasn't sure what she was referring to regarding Jax's past but I agreed with her, he'd tell me when he was ready.

Did she really see all of those things in me? Were they really true? Or was she just trying to talk me into what we'd agreed to do tonight so that she didn't have to go out there alone. I quickly dismissed that notion, Maisie would go out there whether I went with her or not. She was confident and put together, but was that just a mask too?

I'd come to realise that not everything about a person is on the surface for all to see. We all have struggles, we all have insecurities but it's how you wear them that matters. Am I going to sit here wallowing in my self pity or am I going to go out there and show everyone the Piper I wanted to be? I knew Jax loved me just the way I was, flaws and all. He showed me and told me every single day. It was with that realisation that I picked my self loathing up off the floor, lifted my chin and slapped a mask of fake self confidence across my face.

This was for Jax, screw what anyone else thought. Fake it til you make it right?

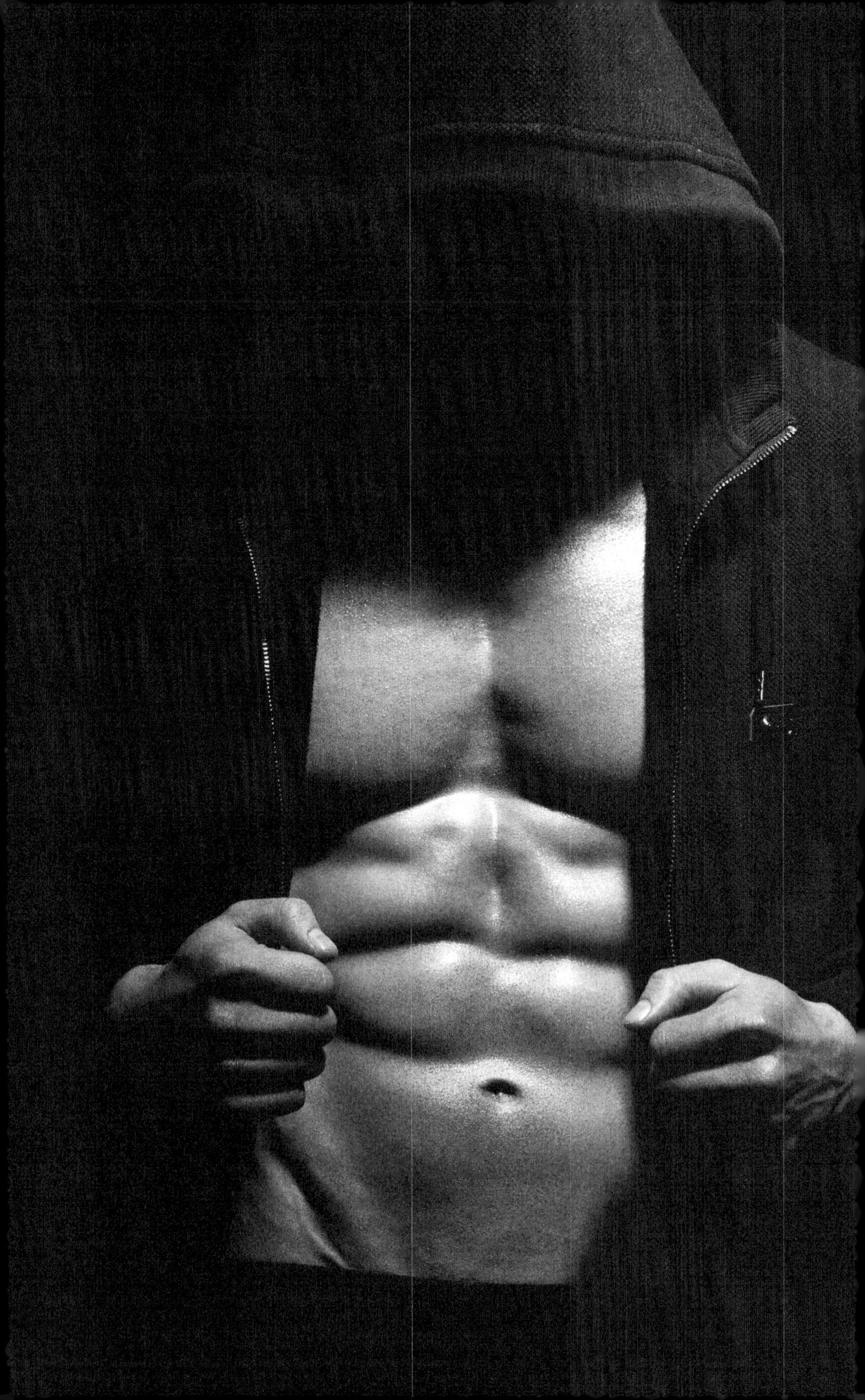

Chapter Fourteen

Jax

That's it, I was done. I had danced my last dance and oiled up my abs for the last time, well the last time in public that was. I was feeling on top of the world, I'd done it. I'd achieved my dream and all of my hard work had paid off. Stripping wasn't for everyone and it wasn't exactly a wholesome way of making money but it had helped me in my time of need and now I could start my real life. With my beautiful Pipes, her daughter and my pub.

I was sat in the main room, surrounded by my mates. The club had been shut down to the public for the rest of the night for my leaving do. The drinks were flowing, the music was pumping and I was beyond happy. Someone was missing though, someone I'd wanted here more than anyone else. It was Friday night though and Piper had Posie tonight, I understood that and I knew that Posie would always come first, as she should. Didn't stop it hurting a little though.

I was deep in conversation with Ace's buddy Mack when my

brother strode across the stage, microphone in hand with the biggest grin on his goofy face. He was up to something, I knew that look. I'd grown to love that look growing up, it meant that today was a good day.

The music quietened down a little as Ace made it to centre stage,

"Good evening everybody and welcome to Jax's leaving do. My names Ace and I'll be your host for the night". He tossed me a cheeky wink. Idiot. I couldn't help but laugh though.

"Tonight, we have a very special treat for Jax. Jax has spent over two years dancing for countless men and women. Shaking his thing and earning his cash, working hard to make his dreams come true. I'm beyond proud of you buddy so I hope you enjoy your treat!". He could barely contain his excitement, he was like a toddler hopped up on sugar.

"Jax ... you've spent years dancing for other people. Tonight I want you to sit back and relax. Enjoy the show brother". He strode off the stage, through the back curtain as the lights dimmed and we were plunged into darkness. Silence filled the room as everybody waited with bated breath to see what would happen. A moment later, my deepest nightmares became a reality as the opening notes to 'Sweet Caroline' blasted through the speakers. Oh hell no, please please please no. My thoughts were quickly silenced and my jaw hit the floor when out shimmied Ace.

Every single person in the audience were stunned silent, the moment seemed to stretch before every single person burst into loud laughter. My twenty seven year old brother shimmied his shoulders and wiggled his hips in possibly the least sexy way I'd ever seen a person move. He was wearing a tiny pair of denim shorts which I was pretty sure belonged to a women. He had a short tie around his neck and a cowboy hat plonked on top of his head. He looked like a complete tool but it was the massive smile plastered across his face that got me.

In this moment he was living his best life. He shimmied and twirled before he dropped to the ground and pumped his hips into the ground before slowly making his way to his feet again. My friends were going absolutely wild, while my jaw was still on the floor as I laughed along with everyone else.

He stroked his hands down his oiled up body, removing his tie as he went. Before moving his hands to his shorts and flicking open the button.

"No no no!" I was on my feet, pleading with my brother not to scar me forever with the sight of his cock. Too late, he whipped his shorts down to his ankles and stood proud as punch. Proud, sweaty and hard as a goddamn hammer. Looks like I wasn't the only Bowman to get off on stripping. I cocked an eyebrow at him with a smirk on my face. He gave me a shoulder shrug in return as he stood with his hands on his hips, his cock reaching up to the skies and his cowboy hat hanging precariously on his head.

The music ended and Ace tossed me a wink before striding off the stage, stark bollock naked. The crowd went wild as my eyes zoned in on ... what the fuck was that?

I slapped a hand to my forehead, "Of course", I muttered to myself. Glaring back at me from the shiny surface of my brothers right arse cheek was a tattoo, not any old tattoo. Nope the bastard had my name tattooed on his arse and was showing it off for all to see. The worst thing was that it didn't look remotely fresh, so when the fuck did my brother think it was a good idea to get the word 'Jax' tattooed on his arse cheek forever.

Fuck my life.

I was pulled from my internal spiral by a new song starting up, I recognised it immediately from one of my favourite movies growing up. The opening bars to 'Will Smith – Men In Black' streamed through the club as the curtain opened again and standing there in a pristine black suit, along with black shades and a bright white shirt was none other than my security guard Mike.

Mike was in his late fifties, had a giant round belly and was probably one of the most serious men I'd ever met. My mind was totally blown when my brothers buddies Hugh and Ryan also came to join him on stage. The three of them strode across the stage, serious faces, ridged shoulders. They stopped at the end of the stage and began to follow the steps of the song.

Will Smith sang 'bounce with me', these three dudes bounced. He told them to slide, they slid. Will told them to 'walk with me' and they walked. It was possibly the most awkward thing I'd ever seen in my entire life. I was embarrassed for them. Each of them looked like they wanted the ground to open up and swallow them whole and I couldn't say I blamed them. Not one of them held an ounce of rhythm as they bounced across the stage. The song was coming to an end, they were all red faced and embarrassed when they came to a stop centre stage, grabbed each side of their pristine suits, ripped the velcro apart as we all watched the remnants fall to the stage.

They were stood in what I can only describe as a tiny strip of red material barely containing their cocks and balls before they turned, baring their g string clad arses before striding back off the stage. The crowd went wild, Mike's wife Isabelle was hooting and hollering up a storm. I was stuck to my seat, what the hell had just happened. As they reached the curtain, Mike turned to look me directly in the eye. He gave me a smirk and a salute and he was gone.

This night was turning out to be possibly the weirdest night of my life.

Fresh drinks were brought around then and I took a moment to pull out my phone to tell Piper what was going on here, she would never believe it.

> **Me:** You will never guess what the hell is happening here baby. I've seen more cocks and balls tonight than I've ever seen before! x

> **Me:** Wish you were here baby x

I really did miss her, she was supposed to be here for my big night. There's no way I'd tell her that though, I know she was sad to miss it.

The next song began to play, I didn't know who the hell was left. It seemed as though everyone was accounted for. The beginning notes to 'Christina Aguilera – Dirty' began to sound through the speakers and it felt like everybody turned to look at me in sync. What was I missing here.

I could see the curtain twitching, somebody was behind it causing it to ripple and wave.

The curtain was pulled back and there stood Maisie, red fiery hair like a bright beacon shining under a single spotlight. Mack's breath hitched in his chest next to me.

"Oh hell no", he was on his feet a second later stalking towards the stage. He didn't get far before Maisie shouted from the stage,

"Sit your arse back down Mackenzie Richards!". He stopped, glared at her for a strong thirty seconds. They were caught in each others stare, Mack glaring, Maisie with a raised eyebrow waiting for her fella to step back in line. He finally relented with a huff and stormed back towards me.

"Do not take a damn piece of clothing off Maisie Richards, that body is for me". I'd never seen him so possessive. Mack was the sweetest, kindest, shyest man I'd ever met. I'd never even heard him raise his voice. He threw himself onto the seat next to me and folded his thick arms across his chest. For a timid guy, he was built like a bloody ox.

Maisie spent a few minutes shaking and grooving around

the stage, strutting her stuff as if nobody was watching. She flicked her long red hair and rolled her hips. Never taking her eyes off of her husband, who despite the glare on his face looked on at her in awe. Much to Mack's delight she didn't remove any clothing and as the song faded out, the breath of relief that left that man was palpable.

Maisie stood at the end of the stage with a soft smile on her face, she wasn't looking at Mack anymore though. She was looking directly at me, before giving me a sweet smile and slowly walking towards the back of the stage. She stopped before turning her gaze back to mine and giving me a soft nod. What was happening? I had a feeling I knew but there was no way I was getting my hopes up. My Pipes was at home with her daughter.

The DJ was going old school now, classic 00's R'n'B filled my ears. 'Usher - My Boo' began playing, Maisie reached a hand behind the curtain and a small hand was placed in hers. My heart began to pound in my chest and I was on my feet in an instant. There was no way, even if Piper were here there was no way that she would get up on that stage in front of all of these people.

My ears were buzzing, my tummy was swirling and my heart was pounding against my chest as that small hand was led out from behind the curtain and my breath stalled in my lungs. Clutching tightly to Maisie's hand was my Pipes, looking completely terrified. She was wearing a tiny little skirt and a skin tight white shirt, flashing me a tantalising amount of boob.

Her hair was beautiful, her bright blue eyes shone through the club, looking like a deer caught in headlights until her gaze landed on mine and she took a deep steadying breath.

I was beyond shocked and in total awe, she was the sexiest damn woman I'd ever seen in my life. It wasn't just her body that was completely sinful, it was her. Her goodness shone out of her and I couldn't be more in love with her if I tried.

It was when she began to move that my breath left my body in a whoosh, she let go of Maisie's hand and sauntered towards me on the stage. Her eyes were locked on mine, as she pretended there was nobody else in the room but us. I could see the tremor in her shoulders as she moved to the music, moving her lips along with the words.

She danced for me, running her hands up and down her gorgeous curvy body. I couldn't take my eyes off of her as my cock grew hard in my jeans and the need to touch her overwhelmed me. My feet were moving before I'd given them permission to as they carried me towards my woman. I jumped up on the stage the second I arrived there and pulled my Pipes into my arms. She was shaking like a leaf and let out a huge sigh of relief as I pulled her into my arms.

"Hi beautiful", I whispered into her ear.

"Hi stud", she whispered back.

"You are so goddamn beautiful Pipes. I'm in awe of you".

"You are?" She looked up into my eyes, uncertainty filling her face.

"I'm so damn proud of you baby, you did that for me?", I murmured in her ear. My voice deep and husky as I tried to regain control over my emotions. I knew that Piper lacked confidence, she was getting better but it was something that had a hold over her. I'd tried to break her free of it since I'd met her, she was the most stunning woman I'd ever met. Not just on the outside but on the inside too.

"I did it for you a-and I d-did it for me too", she stumbled over her words. We had almost forgotten we were still on stage in front of a crowd as we moved along to the music together. I briefly glanced over at the others to see them all dancing along with their significant others.

"I love you baby, more than anything. You are my entire world and you always will be. I am so immensely proud of you Piper, you didn't have to do that for me but I'm so damn proud of you for doing it for yourself".

I brought my lips to hers in a scorching kiss, I pulled her close until we were pressed together tightly. I was rock hard against her tummy and she let me know with a gasp that she could feel me. Her breathing sped up as she snaked a sneaky hand in between us and grasped my stiff cock beneath my jeans.

"Jax, I need you", she muttered breathlessly.

"I need you too baby", I told her. Before grabbing a hold of her hand and pulling her towards the back of the stage in the direction of the private dance rooms. I needed inside of my woman right now. The crowd burst into cheers and hollers as we left. Ace was the loudest of them all as he shouted over the crowd,

"Yes brother, go bone your beauty!". I bowed my head, about to turn my head and apologise to Piper. But she huffed out a quiet chuckle and told me,

"I love your brother", the smile across her face was radiant as pure joy burst from her soul.

"Me too baby, me too".

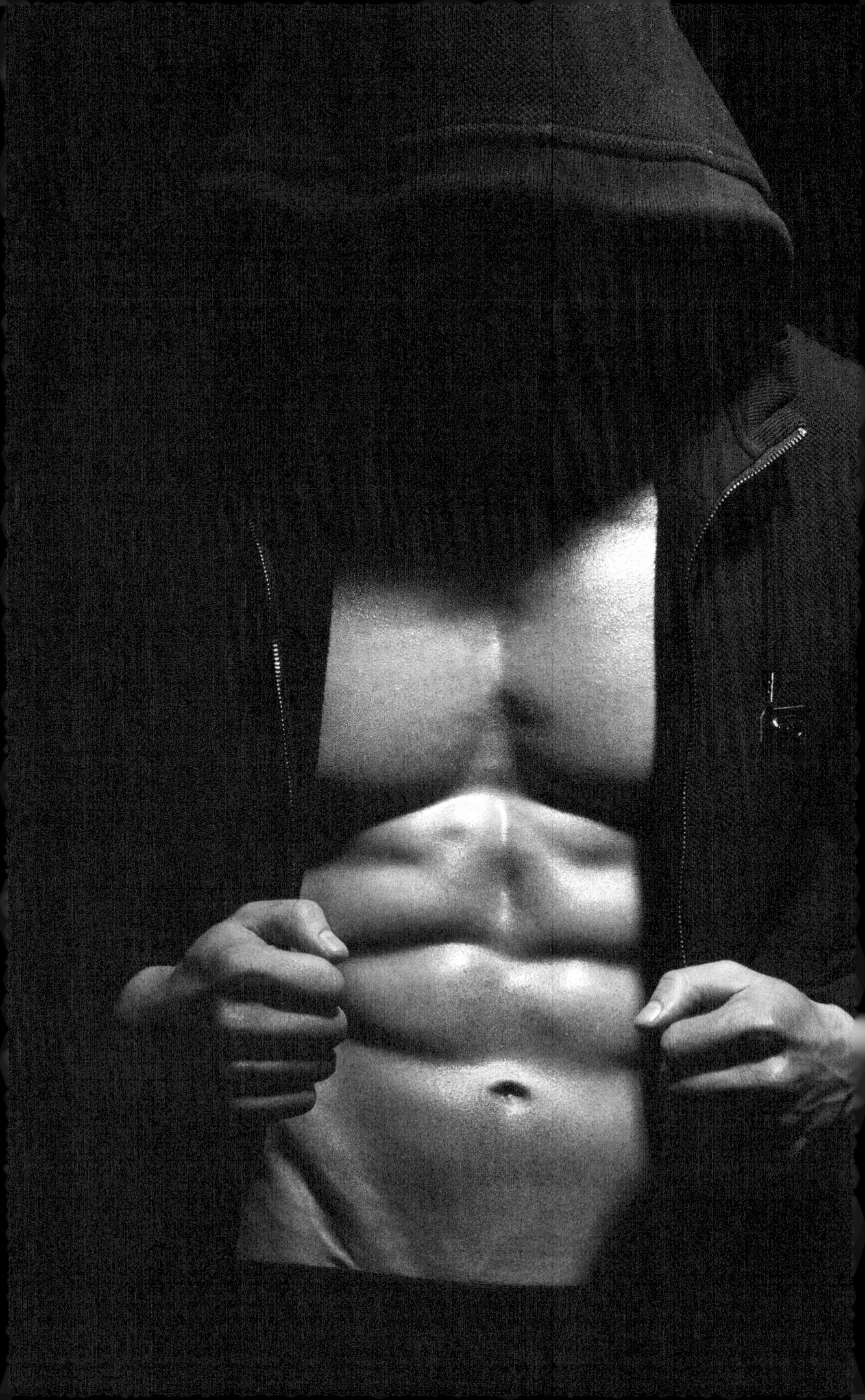

Chapter Fifteen

Piper

Jax took me by the hand and led me backstage into one of the private dance rooms, I'd never been in here and to be completely honest I didn't like the thought of Jax being in here either. But that didn't have to be a worry anymore as this man was all mine, from this moment onwards.

He looked absolutely edible and so young tonight. He was wearing a thin white shirt with sleeves which were rolled up to the elbows, revealing his gorgeous toned and tatted forearms. He had on tight navy jeans and pristine white trainers. On the top of his head was his signature navy backwards hat. He looked absolutely divine. Add that to his chiselled jaw, piercing green eyes, some light stubble and the softest swollen lips and I was about ready to go off like a rocket.

Jax sat me on a chair in the middle of the tiny private stage and moved over to put on some music. I recognised it instantly as the song that was playing the very first time I laid my eyes on this beautiful man.

"You look absolutely stunning tonight Pipes, I'm so proud

of you for getting up on that stage". He told me, voice deep and husky.

"You are?"

"I definitely am, but now it's my turn. I want my very last dance to be for you Pipes", his voice was as smooth as chocolate and I'm pretty sure my panties were about to burst into flames.

"I'd like that too", Jax came to stand directly in front of me. I reached a hand up to stroke down his hard chest and abs. His skin was burning up beneath his shirt and I could feel his heart pounding against his rib cage.

The opening bars of Ginuwine – Pony began to play and it was like we'd been thrown back four months in time. Jax held eye contact with me as he began to move and holy hell this man could move. He moved his hands slowly down his chest and pulled his shirt from his jeans. One by one he flicked the buttons open, slowly revealing his sexy chest and those lickable abs.

He was so unbelievably defined, I wanted to run my tongue across every single one of his grooves, ending at that delicious Adonis belt.

The shirt was pulled free and slid off of his thick shoulders and was thrown across the room.

Next, those thick fingers grasped his belt and made quick work of getting it loose. Whipping it out from his waistband and wrapping it around his fist before placing it on the ground next to the chair. He looked so confident and in control, relaxed and in no rush at all. I on the other hand was about ready to strip naked and climb him like a monkey.

He moved slowly behind me, I could feel the heat radiating off of him. He was still moving to the beat as he leaned down to whisper in my ear.

"You have a choice to make Blondie. Do you want the dance that customers would get or the dance that only my future wife is entitled to?".

His voice and his question sent a shiver of pure heat down my spine, goose bumps rose on my arms as I brought my stare to his. He had a smirk on his handsome face and a question in his eyes. It was the exact same expression he had that very first night. That silent invitation he made, which had made me run for the hills in fear.

I wasn't running anymore though, this man was mine.

"The wife dance ... I want the wife dance". I told him breathlessly. I was so turned on, I'd never been so soaking wet in my life.

"Good answer baby". Jax told me as he brought his huge hands to my shoulders and lowered them down slowly and gently, stopping on my breasts which were heaving for his attention. My nipples were hard as he began to stroke and pinch them above my shirt. He made quick work of untying the knot holding my shirt together. My bare breasts tumbling free into his hands. He danced his way around in front of me, moving to his knees and putting that hot mouth on my body.

He took a nipple into his mouth, licking and nipping until I was writhing beneath him. His thick body taking up every inch between my legs. He reached under my tiny skirt and dragged my thong down my legs before placing them in the back pocket of his jeans.

One minute he was right there in front of me, the next he was disappearing under my skirt and swiping that hot tongue down my centre. I couldn't hold back the moan that left my throat as he devoured me.

"Fuck, you're dripping for me baby. This pussy wants my cock doesn't it?".

"Uh huh, yes!". I moaned.

He placed his hands underneath my arse and pulled my hips right to the edge of the chair. It wasn't the most comfortable position but at this very moment, I really couldn't care less.

He ate me like a starving man, one hand caressing my

boobs, one hand stroking my clit. The heat began to spread through my limbs, his tongue stoking the fire inside of my veins.

"I want you Jax", I purred.

"Then take me out baby, take what's yours". Jax moved to his feet in front of me and moved his hands into my hair as I quickly unzipped his jeans and pulled them down his legs along with his black boxer briefs.

His cock was so hard, his piercing was coated in salty precum which I just couldn't resist as I lowered my head and parted my lips, swiping his smooth tip with my tongue. He tasted delicious as I made quick work of taking him immediately to the back of my throat. He let out a guttural moan as he sank deep inside.

"Take it baby". His hands were firmly in my hair as he began to thrust into my waiting mouth. My tongue caressing him on every down stroke, one hand holding him at the base whilst the other squeezed his balls gently. He grew impossibly hard in my mouth. He was so warm, smooth, hard. I clenched my thighs together to ease the ache building in my core.

He pulled back sharply, "That's enough".

"I want inside you Pipes, I want to fill you".

Jax grabbed me by the hand and led me over the the pole in the middle of the stage. A devious smirk on his face.

"Do you trust me?" He asked gently.

"With my life", I answered instantly.

"That's good baby, what a good girl", he stroked a hand down my cheek as he pushed me to stand directly in front of the pole, my back pushing against the cold metal.

"Arms up, hold on to the pole", he told me as he moved closer to me. That's when I noticed the rolled up belt in his hand. He raised it up and began wrapping it tightly around my wrists and the pole. Not enough to hurt me, just enough to hold me in place.

"Ok?" he asked when I was secure. He looked deeply into

my eyes, I knew he was searching for any signs of discomfort.

"Ok", I told him with a nod. It was true, I trusted this man with my life.

He gave me a sharp nod as he stroked his hands down my body. I was only wearing my tiny skirt and heels now.

"I like you like this baby, you look absolutely stunning". His hands were everywhere, moving from my breasts to my arse, down my stomach to my core.

"Jax, no more teasing. I need you".

"Your wish is my command". He moved forward and placed both hands on my arse and lifted me into the air. The song still playing on repeat, which only made this moment so much hotter.

His hard cock was probing my entrance, I was so dripping wet that he slid against me with ease.

He reached a hand down between us and pushed in deeply, sliding right to the hilt in one thrust. His restraint was gone, his teasing over as he pounded into me sharply. He controlled my hips with his hands, lifting me up and pulling me back down onto him. His thick biceps straining with the movement.

"Fuck baby, you're so tight. Look at you taking me so well". His eyes were glued to the part of us that was connected and so was mine. Fuck that's so hot.

Sweat was trickling down his chest, beading on his forehead too. He reached up to remove his hat as I almost growled at him.

"Leave the hat!". He answered me with a smirk in return.

"Fan of the backwards hat huh?".

"Fuck yes!". I was so close as I tried to ride him the best I could, my sweaty hands sliding against the pole as I fought to hold on. He was relentless, his hips pumping, his muscles contracting. He leaned his head forwards towards my collar bone and took a sharp bite of my skin. That's what sent me reeling. One bite and I was soaring, heat flooded my core, pressure built and I exploded, soaking him in the process. White lights flashed behind my eyes, buzzing sounded in my ears. I couldn't even hear my own screams but I knew I was making them.

   Jax wasn't far behind as his eyes rolled into the back of his head and he froze, hands tightly gripping my arse cheeks, buried to the hilt as he pumped me full of warmth. He spilled deep inside of me with a groan.

   After long minutes of catching our breath and coming back down to earth. Jax pulled out. His hot come trickling down my inner thighs, he noticed of course. He used his finger to scoop it up and push it back inside of me.

   "I belong in here, not in a puddle on the floor. This is mine". He used two thick fingers to push back inside of me. I was so sensitive I couldn't help but clench down around him.

   He stepped forward, unclasped the belt and placed a soft kiss on my mouth, whispering against my lips.

   "Best last dance ever, future wifey".

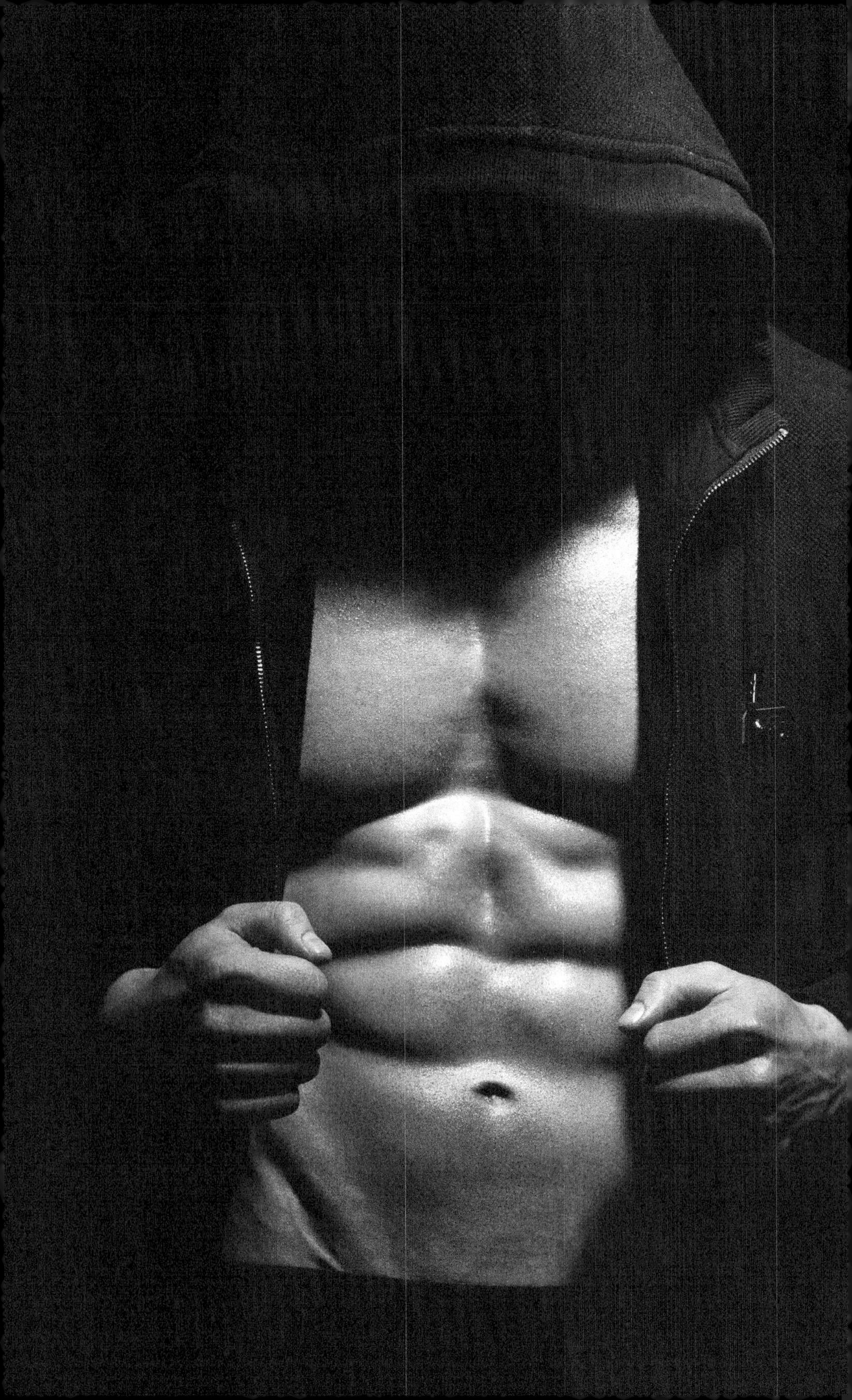

Chapter Sixteen

Jax

It had been three weeks since my last night at the club and three weeks of hard work. The guys had helped me to totally revamp the pub, fresh coats of paint, a custom made bar and tables, we had even added a small stage in the corner in the hope of attracting some talent.

Tonight was opening night and I was beyond excited to get my dream started, I was ready to make something of myself. Growing up, I'd constantly been told that I'd amount to nothing. I was worthless and would end up in the same rut my parents had landed in. My fucked up childhood already meant that I hadn't done very well in school, Ace hadn't either. Thankfully we were able to turn things around in college, once we were free from our parents.

I hated my father for what he'd done to us, my mother too but as I'd gotten older I'd grown to understand that she'd become a product of him. She was as much his victim as we had been, she couldn't have gotten out if she'd tried to.

When you spend years and years of your life being abused and drugged, tormented and beaten on a daily basis, it's easy to turn into a version of yourself that you don't like. A version that cannot protect the children you brought into the world. My mother had shut her feelings off, she shut down to be able to tolerate the disgusting things that happened to her. I didn't blame her for leaving us anymore, I didn't hold it against her. Everybody has a breaking point and she had reached hers. I forgave her, but I'd never forgive my father.

   I think that's why I wanted to build my own pub. I wanted to run it in a way that was supportive of those in the community. I wanted to create a safe space for people to find refuge, I had big plans for the future to create a space out back for anybody who needed it. I didn't just want 'Jax's' to be a place where people came to get wasted, I wanted it to be a place to come when you needed someone to listen. Sometimes a broken person just needs to be heard and I was determined to listen.

   Opening night had been a huge success, Piper and Ace had both helped me behind the bar and it was an absolute smash. If Ace ever gave up the firefighting then he was born to be behind that bar. He came across as a completely unserious goofball, but like me he'd seen things in his life that made him wise. He was the kind of person you could find yourself opening up to, without even realising it.

   "Buddy, I'm so proud of you. This place is amazing", Ace told me before bringing me in for a hug.

"I couldn't have done it without you brother", the words brought a lump to my throat, I tried to swallow it down before continuing.

"Thank you for saving me", my green eyes clashed with his big brown ones. I could see the emotion reflected back at me as he held me close again. He heaved a big breath before telling me,

"I'll always save you Jax, you're my other half. We've been through some shit but we both came out as better men because we have each other. Bowman Brothers forever". He ruffled my hair as he stood back and discreetly swiped a tear from his cheek.

"Bowman Brothers forever", I echoed.

Later that night when Piper and I were snuggled together in bed, both tired and satiated from our celebratory sex, I decided it was time to open up my heart and tell her my story. I trusted her with my life, I trusted that she wouldn't hurt me, I'd found the other half of my soul.

"Piper ... can I tell you something?"

"Of course baby, always", she turned those big blue eyes to look at me, laying her head on my chest and stroking a hand across my jaw.

I felt safe, I felt secure. That is what made me open up and tell Piper about my life. I told her about my parents and how we'd grown up, I told her about the abuse and the torment inflicted on us. I told her about my mother's death and my father's arrest and I told her how my brother had saved me.

It was only when both of our tears had dried and she held me close in her arms, telling me how much she loved me and wanted a future with me, that I finally felt accepted.

I wasn't just 'Jax The Stripper' anymore, or 'Jax The Broken Boy', I was simply Jax. Piper saw me, accepted me, fixed all of my broken parts and smoothed all of my jagged edges and loved me anyway.

After twenty four years on this earth, I finally felt that it was ok to just be …. me.

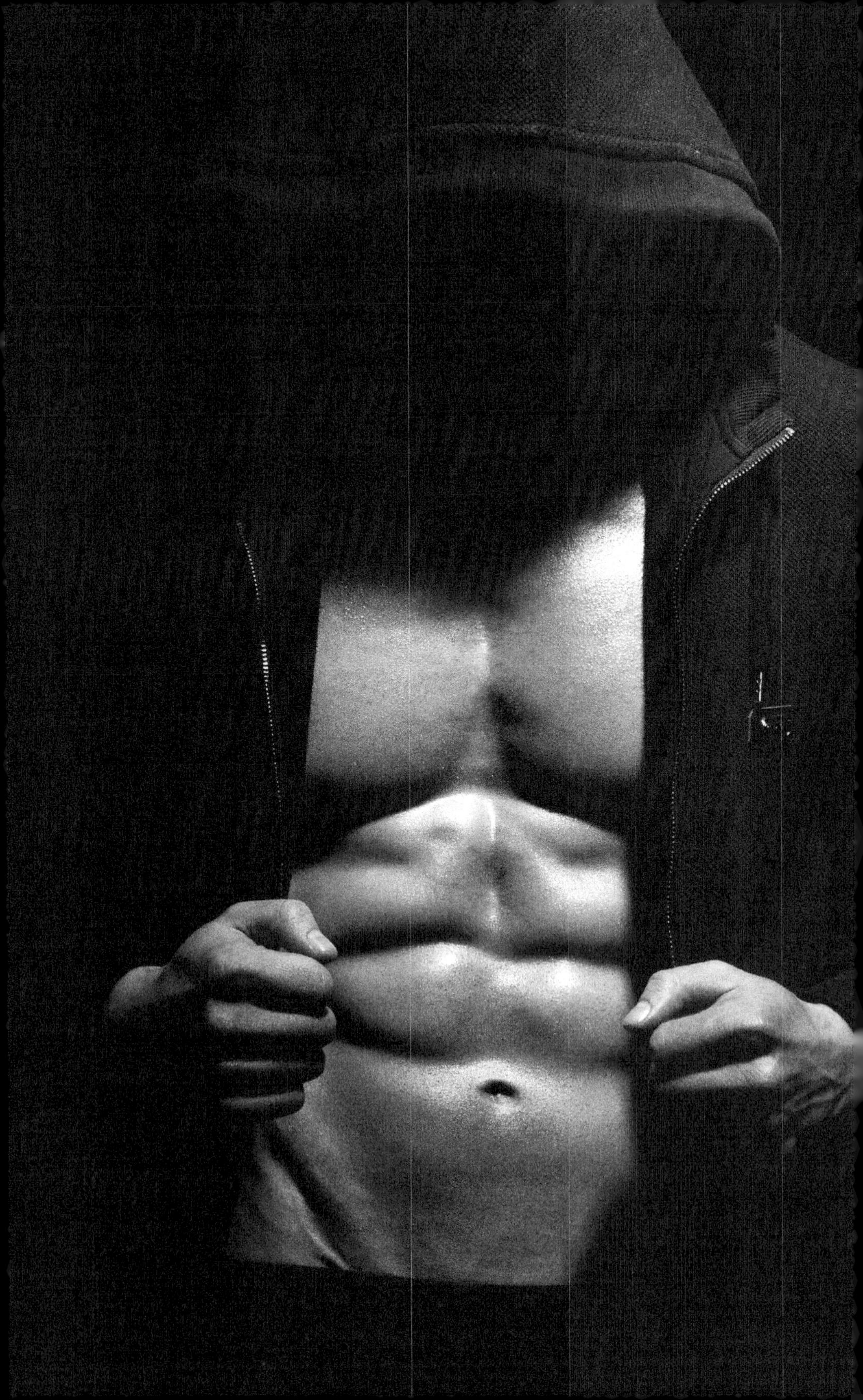

Epilogue

Posie

Two Years Later

Today was the day that my Mum had been waiting for, she didn't know it yet but her mind was about to be blown! Now, I'm only twelve but even I could understand how much today was going to mean to her.

Mum met Jax about two and a half years ago, he's a lot younger than her but who the hell cares. I know I don't, he's pretty cool. He buys me gifts all the time and takes me places when I ask him to. That's not the most important thing though, he makes my Mum happy.

She was never really happy with my Dad, I used to hear them fighting all the time, especially because Dad kept kissing other women. Jax wasn't like that, my Mum was his favourite person in the world and I knew that I was a favourite of his too. I'd never felt left out and I'd never felt unloved by him, he was the perfect step dad.

Today was going to be a really special day, Jax was going to ask my Mum to marry him and she was going to say yes. I couldn't wait for her to say yes, I'd get to wear a pretty dress and get my hair and make up done!

Mum also had a secret that she was keeping, I was pretty sure that she might tell us today. I already knew though, I just hadn't told her.

So, Uncle Ace was coming to pick me and Mum up in the nosh wagon. I had no idea why he called it that, it was always a mess inside though so I'm guessing maybe he ate his dinner in there a lot.

"Hi honeys", he called out as he stopped outside the pub, "Your chariot awaits". We quickly clambered in and then we were off.

We had lived with Jax in the pub for about a year now, I had my own room which Jax had let me decorate however I'd wanted. Uncle Mack had even made me a special desk to do all of my homework on.

We drove for around forty minutes, Ace sang along to the radio like he was a popstar the entire time, I'd tried to sing along with him but the superstar outshone me the whole journey here. Travelling in the nosh wagon was definitely an experience that's for sure and Uncle Ace might just be my favourite person in the whole world, don't tell Mum and Jax that though.

We pulled up at the beach. It was a beautiful sunny day, the sun was reflecting off of the sea and the sand was soft and smooth beneath our feet as we took off our shoes and walked towards Jax. We could see him in the distance, he was wearing his normal everyday outfit of jeans, white shirt and backwards hat. Mum loved it when he dressed like that. She was wearing a beautiful baby blue polka dot summer dress, I'd made sure she dressed up a little bit without giving too much away.

As we got closer to Jax, he looked past my Mum and gave me a gentle nod. Ace and I stopped where we were and let my Mum move closer until he pulled her into his arms. We couldn't hear what they were saying from where we were but I could see the massive smiles on both of their faces.

Mum's friend Maisie was hiding behind the beach hut nearby snapping picture after picture, I say hiding but she was pretty obvious. Her hair was so bright and wild, flapping around her head like she was in a tornado.

Uncle Ace and I stood watching Mum and Jax for ages before he finally got down on one knee and asked her the special question. He had asked me if it was ok about a month ago and of course I said yes. Jax was the best thing that had happened to her since she had me, that's what she always said anyway.

Uncle Ace placed a hand around my shoulder and pulled me into his side,

"You ok there kiddo?" he asked.

"Yeah ... I am".

"Nice to see them happy isn't it?" he replied. Mum had just said yes to Jax, well actually she shouted it so loudly we could hear it from all the way over here.

"It's the best thing in the world, my Mum used to be sad all the time when she was with my Dad. Jax makes her heart happy and that makes my heart happy".

"You're a special girl you know that Po? Not a lot of kids would be happy seeing their parents move on".

"I don't feel like I'm missing out. I'm getting another parent and a pretty cool one at that".

"I love you Po, look after Jaxy for me won't you?". He moved his hand from my shoulder and gripped my hand in his before turning back to Mum and Jax just in time to see the shocked expression plastered across Jax's face. I smirked to myself as Ace asked,

"Wonder what that's all about. Do you know kiddo?". He

looked down at me, I looked back up at him and asked,
   "You got space in the nosh wagon for another one? You're going to be an Uncle again".

The End

What's Next...

*Have you read Hugh and Sophie's story in Lost and Found?
Out now on Amazon.
Follow along on Instagram for updates on further releases.
Find me at c.smith_books*

Finding Forever Series

The series will be as follows:

Book One: Lost And Found – Hugh And Sophie's Novel.

Book Two: Found And Flirty – Mack And Maisie's Novella.

Book Three: Lost And Forever – Ace And Elodie's Novel.

Book Four: Found And Free – Ryan And Freya's Novella.

Book Five: Lost And Forgiven – Kit And Lily's Novel.

Acknowledgements

Rich, you have given me the opportunity to follow my dreams and I'll forever be grateful to you. You also gave me the two very best people in the world, our children. You made my dreams come true a very long time ago.

Mum and Dad, thank you for always supporting me and being proud of whatever I choose to do. Mum, thanks for talking me down when I have a panic and consider throwing in the towel. The saying is true, you're never too old to need your Mum.

Shan, I hope you enjoyed your cameo!

Kerry, thanks for being my BETA reader and always being so excited to read my stories.

My ARC readers, I can't thank you enough for all of your support and lovely comments. Your likes, tags and shares give me a massive boost. So thank you.

About The Author

C.Smith was born and raised in Hastings in the South Of England, she now resides a little further along the coast in Hampshire. When she's not writing, she can usually be found with a nose in someone else's book.

C.Smith is happily married with two young children. She loves anything creative, whether it be writing, crochet or playing around with vinyl.

She is currently working full time as a romance author and creating fun merchandise for her online store https://csmithbooks.onlineweb.shop/

For more updates, visit her website linked above, sign up to her newsletter to receive her free novella or find her on Instagram at c.smith_books

Printed in Great Britain
by Amazon